UNSEASONED ADVENTURER

HALF-WIZARD THORDRIC BOOK 3

KATHRYN WELLS

1

VEY'S WISH

Thordric's brow creased as he gazed at his notes, flicking through them with annoyance. He'd been working on his dishwashing spell for weeks, and though he'd cracked the first part to make the plates clean themselves after he'd finished eating, getting the magical lacquer to stick to plates that didn't come from the Wizard Council was proving far more difficult than he'd first thought.

Unfortunately, it was the lacquer that made the spell work. It was composed of a special powder that, upon detection of cold waste substances, would force them all up into a great floating mass of muck which then levitated itself into the nearest waste bin. Both practical and entertaining, Thordric had thought, but without a way to make the lacquer stick to normal plates, there was no way anyone other than the council could use it.

This was one of the reasons why Thordric's mood that morning was particularly grim. No matter how much he adjusted the ingredients or the mixing time, he still couldn't get the lacquer to like the feel of ordinary crockery. True, turning the powder into a lacquer was certainly a step up from when he'd tried to use it raw (which had either failed to work or made the mass of waste food fly at the diner's face), but it still flat out rejected normal plates and dishes despite there being no real difference between those and the Wizard Council's ones. Perhaps it was the magical residue left on the Wizard Council's plates that made the lacquer like them so much.

He jotted the idea down in his notebook, but then realised that he also needed to find something that would rinse and dry the plates after the waste food had disappeared. Absently tugging out several strands of his thick dark hair, he thought back to all the trouble he'd had with spells before. There had been many times when he'd thought his magic wasn't good enough, and in each case, he'd surprised himself by making things work. But this time...no, he wouldn't let despair sink in yet. He could do this; he was just stuck in a rut at the moment. That was all.

The Wizard Council had been Thordric's home for six years now, ever since he'd helped solve the murder case of High Wizard Kalljard and revealed the High Wizard's terrible plans to eradicate all the half-wizards in Dinia. Even though Thordric was only twenty-one, the youngest Council member of all time, he was treated with respect by the council's new leader, High Wizard Vey, something that many of the older wizards still muttered about behind his back.

Not to mention that unlike most of the wizards at the council, both he and Vey were half-wizards which had caused quite a stir when Vey had revealed this fact at Thordric's initiation ceremony, because, thanks to Kalljard's lies over the many years he'd been head of the Wizard Council, everyone had believed that half-wizards were dangerous and couldn't control their magic.

Of course, it was true that full wizards came from families

that had never had any magic in them before (thus they supposedly received all the potential magic of that bloodline) and half-wizards came from families that had already produced a wizard, but as to their magic being dangerous, Thordric had disproved that many times. In fact, he'd shown the council that the only difference between full and half-wizard magic was that full wizards were trained how to use theirs from an early age, whereas half-wizards received no training at all and were left to work out things for themselves, sometimes with hazardous results.

It was to put an end to all the prejudice against half-wizards that he and Vey had reformed the council, accepting half-wizards to be trained at the Wizard Council Training Facility as early as full wizards were. It'd taken a lot of work, but now the hatred for them was dissolving, allowing the people of Dinia to live together peacefully no matter what their lineage.

So now Thordric had much more time to focus on making new spells, which was why he'd started work on his dishwashing spell, trying to make a way for the busy people of Dinia to clean their dishes instantly so they could spend time doing other things.

A knock came at his door, making him jump and hit his head on the bookshelf above his desk. He yelped, and the door came crashing open to reveal Kal, the teenage wizard that Thordric had been put in charge of three years ago, staring at him with concern.

'Thordric, what happened? Are you—'

'I'm fine, Kal,' Thordric grumbled irritably, rubbing his head. 'Was there something you needed?'

'No, not me. It's High Wizard Vey, he's sent you an official summons,' Kal said, eying the notebook on Thordric's desk.

Thordric saw him and shut it quickly. Kal had a habit of

picking up bits of magic theory from here and there and trying to make them work by himself, something that most often ended in disaster. 'Vey?' Thordric said, raising an eyebrow. 'An official summons? Sounds serious, I hope he hasn't come down with something.'

Kal laughed nervously. Thordric knew the young wizard still wasn't quite used to the way he and Vey treated each other so informally, though he'd made sure to tell him exactly what they'd been through together, and that Thordric's own mother had married Vey's uncle some years ago, making them bonded closely by family as well as by friendship.

'I suppose I'd better go and see what he wants,' Thordric said, getting up and putting his notebook in the desk drawer, locking it, and placing the key in his pocket. He didn't miss the look of disappointment on Kal's face as he did so, but he chose not to comment. Instead, he strolled out of the room and down the various twists and turns of the council's crescent-moon-shaped building until he reached the staircase leading up to Vey's room.

Kal had been following him closely, but now Thordric turned to him. 'Perhaps it would be best if you continued with your studies,' he said, not unkindly. 'Try the painting spell again. See if you can do it in colour rather than black and white. I'll come along and check it later.'

Kal mumbled a meek reply of thanks and scurried off down the hall. Thordric raised his eyebrow again; it was unusual for Kal not to argue with him about practicing a spell that didn't involve explosions. He shrugged and carried on up the slim staircase until he got to the door at the top, knocking politely.

'Enter,' Vey's voice came, strangely formal.

Thordric did so and found that Vey's bedchamber had been turned into what looked like a meeting room. There were five wizards seated in a circle, with Vey sitting the furthest away from him, and he also saw that Inspector Jimmson, from Jard Town's local stationhouse (and incidentally, his own stepfather) was there, too.

The inspector nodded to Thordric as their eyes met but stayed silent. Thordric surveyed Vey and the other wizards. Vey was wearing robes of a deep blue, with the Wizard Council's symbol of a book and potion bottle in front of a half-moon stitched across the entire front. Thordric had only seen Vey wear these robes on official occasions, such as the Winter Celebration and other public appearances. Never had he worn them within the council before. He'd always told Thordric that they were too oppressive and heavy to wear on a regular basis. Thordric looked him in the eyes and Vey's mouth twitched ever so slightly, as though he was fighting the urge to smile. The rest of the wizards, all of whom Thordric knew well and spoke to regularly, were also wearing their official robes, and had the same expression as Vey.

Thordric looked down at his own robes, noting how faded and patchy they were, and blushed. When Kal had told him it was an official summons, he hadn't expected it to be as formal as this.

There was an empty chair directly opposite Vey, and, now nervous, Thordric took it. As he did so, a ripple of exhales ran through the circle, but as he looked at everyone, he thought he might have imagined it.

'Wizard Thordric, you have been summoned here today to bear witness to High Wizard Vey's *Wishes Upon Death or Retirement*,' one of the wizards to Vey's right said in a clear voice.

Thordric blinked at him. Wishes upon death or retirement? What did they mean? Was Vey ill?

He was about to jump up and ask when Vey held up his hand. 'This is purely a formality. All will be explained in due course,' he said calmly, a hint of his normal voice rolling in. He gestured for the wizard who had spoken to continue.

The wizard coughed to clear his throat. 'As a wizard who has contributed substantially to the objectives of the Wizard Council, it is our duty and our pleasure to inform you, Wizard Thordric, that his reverence, High Wizard Vey, wishes you to become his successor in the event of his death or if he is unable to continue his role as High Wizard successfully.'

Thordric tugged at his ears, unsure if he had heard him correctly.

The wizard continued. 'Do you accept his reverence's most gracious offer?'

Apparently, he had heard correctly. Suddenly, the room seemed to be unstable, and he fell off his chair with a crash. He tried to get up, but the floor swam underneath him, and his head hit the ground in a faint.

'I knew this would happen,' Vey's voice said somewhere above him. 'He's not the sort of person you can spring things on. If I'd hinted my intentions to him a few weeks ago, maybe he would have suspected something like this and been more prepared.'

'Nonsense, Eric. The boy has to grow up at some point. After all, he's a young man now; he needs to prime himself for things like this.'

Thordric scrunched up his brow, his eyes too heavy to open. Someone had called Vey 'Eric'. The only person who did that was Vey's mother, Lizzie.

'But, Mother, was it really necessary for all the formality?' Vey protested. 'I think it was that more than anything that surprised him.'

'Well, perhaps it was a step too far,' Lizzie said thoughtfully. 'But I have noticed that you have been neglecting the formalities of the council of late. You must keep them going, Eric, otherwise the people won't take you seriously.'

Thordric managed to laugh. Taking Vey seriously as head of the council was quite hard, for he usually drifted about as casually as anyone, and frequently gave his guards the slip simply to be free of them for a few hours. It wasn't how most people thought the High Wizard should act at all.

'So, you're awake then, boy,' Lizzie said, propping his head up on a plump pillow that smelt of rose petals and nutmeg.

With effort, he opened his eyes and saw her and Vey looking at him. They were in Lizzie's townhouse, and Vey was sitting in a wicker armchair opposite the sofa that Thordric was lying on, his face matching the few grey flecks that had started to appear in his short beard, while she was standing over Thordric, a questioning look on her face.

'Come now, boy, what was that all about? Surely you must have had some idea of what Eric intended for you?' she said, handing him a cup of chocolate and blueberry tea. He took it gratefully and sat up.

'I...no, not really. I know you both think a lot of me, and I'm grateful for that, but...High Wizard? You really want me to be the next one?' he asked.

'Of course,' Vey said. 'Out of all the wizards at the council, you are the only one who has truly helped me to sort out the mess that Kalljard left us in and improved the spells and potions we make so that they really help people instead of being gimmicks. I've spoken to everyone, and we all agree – you're the best choice we've got. Even Wizard Ayek agreed, and you know how much he dislikes you...and me, come to that. Mind you, that might have been because I threatened to have Hamlet give a talk on his latest archaeological finds if he refused.'

Thordric snorted. Hamlet was a young archaeologist he'd

met three years ago on his travels to Neathin Valley, and he was so enthusiastic about his work that he would talk about it for hours and hours if anyone let him.

Vey smiled. 'But why are you deciding this now?' Thordric asked him. 'Surely you're not stepping down yet?'

The thought of taking over from Vey so soon made Thordric's insides jump about quite violently.

Vey shook his head. 'No, I think I can manage for at least another twenty years, but I thought I should put it in my *Wishes Upon Death or Retirement* to be on the safe side. After all,' he said with a grin, 'with Kal running around causing explosions everywhere, you never know what will happen.'

Thordric pulled a pained expression. 'Speaking of Kal, where is he? Is he still back at the council?'

'He is. I checked on him after you fainted. He was practicing the painting spell like you told him to. There were a few scorch marks on the wall, though. Maybe I should send him to the Training Facility a few times a week. I know you're trying your best with him, but perhaps he needs a bit more discipline...'

They all looked at each other. Kal wasn't a bad student, but he was very impatient and constantly wanted to learn new spells before he'd fully grasped the simpler ones, and once or twice Thordric had given in to his complaints and taught him some. If one of the wizards at the Training Facility could do better, then Thordric would give them a medal.

2

HAMLET'S DISCOVERY

Two days later, once Thordric had recovered sufficiently and finally relented to being the next High Wizard once Vey stepped down, Kal knocked hard on his door again.

'Come in, Kal,' he said, not even bothering to look up from his notes.

'How did you know it was me?' Kal asked, eyeing Thordric suspiciously. Thordric grinned.

'No one else would knock on my door quite that hard... well, Vey might, but only if it was really urgent, and since he has his long-distance communicator with him all the time, he usually calls me on that,' Thordric said, prodding his own long-distance communicator. It was a small box with a button sticking out of the back and, curiously, a small, blue flower poking out of a hole on the top. The communicators had been Thordric's invention, having made them for his journey to Neathin Valley three years before, and relied on the strong connection between parts of a plant that have been divided.

It was in Neathin Valley that he'd first met Kal, who had accidentally managed to cause one of the biggest disasters that

Dinia had ever seen. Once the damage had all been rectified, Vey had thought it best for Kal to be given some serious instruction on how to use his magic, nominating Thordric to take him on. But even now Thordric thought that might have been a mistake. He barely had control over his own magic, let alone trying to teach someone else.

'Oh,' Kal said, a little sheepishly. 'I thought you would like to know that Hamlet's back. He's in the dining hall now, talking to Vey. He seemed very excited about something.'

Thordric chuckled. 'It doesn't take much to make him excited. Last month I showed him the bones of a goat that Vey had found tucked away in one of the rooms full of Kalljard's old junk, and he leapt on them and started telling me they must be from a species that's extinct. He went on about it for days.'

'Were they from a goat species that's now extinct?' Kal asked, tugging at his short dreadlocks. They were a recent addition, because Thordric had gotten fed up with him for leaving trails of hair all over the bathroom floor.

'Well, yes, I think they were, actually,' said Thordric dismissively. 'But anyway, I'd better go and see him before he comes rambling in here and knocks over my work.'

Kal sniggered and left the room with Thordric in tow, making their way to the dining hall. The hall had been freshly decorated that morning, as it was now the custom for the colour to be changed every month –an idea of Vey's to help make it more inviting not only for the council wizards, but for anyone visiting.

As they walked through the door, they saw Hamlet's unmistakeable blond hair and pale face grinning at them from one of the tables at the far back of the room. Despite how much sun he always got from spending time doing archaeological field work, his skin never turned darker than a glass of milk. He waved to them and pulled out their chairs, but Kal mumbled an excuse about leaving a potion brewing and dashed off to drain it.

'Nice to see you back, Hamlet,' Thordric said as he took his seat. He eyed the room. 'I thought Vey was in here with you?'

'Oh, he was, but he's just gone to pack,' Hamlet said cheerily, watching the teapot Thordric had summoned from the serving table pour him a large cup of tea. He took it and sniffed. 'Oh good, I like this one—'

'Sorry, did you just say Vey has gone to *pack*?' Thordric choked.

'Yes, why?' Hamlet said, taking a sip of his tea, oblivious as to why the head of the Wizard Council suddenly up and leaving was a strange idea.

'Where's he going?' Thordric pressed.

'He's coming with me. We're leaving right after dinner. Anyway, have a look at what I've discovered,' he said, opening his bag, which was so over-filled that Thordric'd had to put a strengthening spell on the seams last time he had seen him. Hamlet pulled out several large notebooks filled with sketches and diagrams, and something that looked like an overlarge mushroom made from vine roots and glass. He was about to tell him about it when he saw Thordric's face. 'Did you want to know where we're going?'

Thordric tried not to let out a growl of frustration. 'If you wouldn't mind.'

'It's not far from here; only takes a few days to get there. I was on my way back when Kal contacted me on the long-distance communicator, saying that you'd had a fainting spell and he needed a particular plant to make a potion for your recovery. I was near a forest at the time and happened to see the plant he described to me. I suppose I got rather distracted and decided to have a look around. That's when I saw them; two strange figures carved out of some kind of crystal. I didn't have time to look at them properly, but they were fascinating. When I told Vey that I was going back to check them out, he decided to come with me.'

Thordric's eyes narrowed. 'It's unusual for him to go on a trip so spontaneously.' He scratched his chin, feeling that there was stubble there. His mother had made him shave the week before for his twin little sisters' birthday party, but shaving was something that he felt was a waste of time. Plus, when he had a beard, he could tug at it when he was thinking.

'Well, I think he mentioned something about Lizzie wanting to come over for tea tomorrow, but he thinks she wants to check up on how the council's running from the inside. Now that he's allowed the public to come in any time they want, she wants to make sure it's tidy and that any dangerous magic going on is kept away from people.'

'That does sound like Lizzie. At least it explains Vey's behaviour,' Thordric said, unable to suppress his grin.

Hamlet looked puzzled. 'What do you mean? He's very excited about what I've found, I'm sure he's leaving so soon because he can't wait to see for himself.'

Thordric opened his mouth but closed it again quickly. He wasn't sure he had the heart to tell Hamlet how wrong he was.

True to their word, Hamlet and Vey left after dinner that evening, though not before Hamlet had given Thordric an extensive breakdown of everything he'd discovered on his latest expedition.

Instead of nodding off as usual whenever Hamlet talked for a long time, Thordric listened with genuine interest. It appeared that Hamlet had found out a lot about the cultures that'd lived in the area before Kalljard had taken over and built Jard Town a thousand years ago.

Due to Kalljard's influence over the people, much of history before that had been forgotten or purposely concealed, and it was only now he was gone that archaeologists like Hamlet were given free rein to dig around wherever they wanted. One of the most interesting theories Hamlet was working on was that there used to be women born with magic as well as men, which was completely unheard of. However, though he'd found plenty of evidence for this to be true, what Hamlet couldn't fathom was why it no longer happened.

'Perhaps you'll find that out later,' Vey suggested, trying to herd Hamlet out the large double doors. He waved goodbye to Thordric, and sternly told his guards that if they came after him, he would force them to drink some of the potion that Kal was currently working on. None of them took even a step after that and closed the doors reluctantly behind him.

Thordric lingered in the hall, watching the guards mutter under their breath as they went away to their rooms, before heading back to his own. He sat down at his desk, taking his notebook out of the drawer, but it was no use. His eyes were so heavy that he simply couldn't bring himself to do anymore work that night. Not to mention the dread he felt, now that Vey had left him in charge while he was gone.

Lying down on the bed, he buried his head in his pillow, ready to sleep, but then a thought occurred to him. Why had Kal contacted Hamlet on the long-distance communicator instead of going to look for whatever plant he needed himself?

Thordric's rule was that if Kal wanted to make any kind of potion, he had to research and collect all the ingredients himself. And where had Kal been at dinner? Now that Thordric thought about it, he hadn't seen him anywhere. Indeed, Vey wouldn't have made such a comment about his potions if he had actually been there. Upsetting people was the last thing that Vey did.

Sighing, Thordric got up, deciding to investigate Kal's whereabouts. Unfortunately, he tripped over his trailing bed sheets and plummeted into the bookshelf again, hitting his head a mere inch from where he'd hit it last time, but much harder. He muttered a string of colourful curses that no one but Vey and Hamlet knew he knew and took a vial of bright orange potion out from one of his drawers. He unscrewed the cap and tipped a splodge onto his fingers, and then massaged it into the bump that was now forming on his head. The potion was thick and slightly greasy, but it took the pain away almost instantly.

He put the potion back in his drawer and then eyed his bedcovers angrily, before leaving the room and turning left up the corridor towards the main part of the building. Kal's room wasn't actually in the council building at all but was located at the Training Facility which had been built facing the back of the council, completely hidden from view by a large wall of thick trees. The idea was that if any of the wizards in training did something wrong, it wouldn't alarm any of the townspeople walking past.

As Kal wasn't actually a student at the Facility, when he made a mistake, it was up to Thordric to see that no one had been hurt in the process. On the brighter side, Kal hadn't caused any major explosion for the past two months.

Thordric reached the door to the training Facility and knocked, hearing it echo through the halls behind for almost a minute. When the door finally opened, a wizard dressed in an apron and carrying a mop and bucket stood there. When he saw Thordric, however, he almost shut it again in fear.

'Hello, Rarn,' Thordric said to him cheerfully. 'Can I come in?'

The wizard called Rarn didn't answer but continued to stare at Thordric as though he thought he might attack him. Thordric couldn't blame him; when he'd first joined the council, Rarn had been less than welcoming and had also kept Kall-jard's plan to eradicate all the half-wizards a secret from everyone else. So Thordric had done the proper thing and set a stone statue chasing after him for nearly three days.

Vey had then decided to make it Rarn's job to clean the Training Facility on a daily basis. He hadn't shown himself at the council since.

Taking Rarn's silence to mean 'yes', Thordric stepped into the hall. He thought about asking him where Kal's room was but figured that would merely lead to more silence.

He decided to take the passage to the right. That was where Kal's room had been the last time Thordric had been there, but as the students changed rooms every year, he knew that it was probably somewhere different now. However, much to his luck, it appeared that Kal had been moved just a few doors down from his old room and happened to open the door as Thordric walked past.

They both jumped violently.

'Thordric! What are you doing down here this late?' Kal asked once they'd regained their composure.

'What do you think?' Thordric replied, rolling his eyes. 'I was looking for you, of course.' He glanced down, his eyes latching on to Kal's hands. They were heavily bandaged.

Kal hid them hastily behind his back.

'What happened?' Thordric demanded. 'Are you hurt?'

'I...had a bit of an accident with that potion I was brewing,' he said, staring at the floor. His dreadlocks hung in front of his eyes, shielding them from Thordric's stare. 'When I was cutting up the ingredients, I, uh, accidentally cut myself a few times with the knife. And when I rushed back earlier to drain the potion off, it splashed on my hands, and went into the cuts.'

'What potion was it? I don't remember asking you to try any this week,' Thordric said.

Kal avoided his gaze even more, and then said quietly, 'It was to get rid of acne. One of my friends has got it really badly.'

Thordric had surmised as much, though he knew it was really Kal's acne that was bad. If only he'd asked, Thordric would have given him some potion from his stores. 'Let me see them,' he said.

Kal reluctantly held up his hands. Using his magic, Thordric unwrapped the bandages quickly...and gaped. Kal's hands were covered in what looked like small craters, and one of them had sunk into his skin so much that it had almost reached the bone.

'Come with me,' Thordric said, grabbing Kal by the arm and marching him out of the building.

They bolted back to Thordric's chambers, where he dug around in his drawers for more of the orange potion he'd used earlier. He found it and spread it thickly over Kal's hands. 'This will only reduce the holes a fraction, but the pain should stop,' he said.

Kal winced as the cold potion touched his hands.

'Right, then,' Thordric continued, standing up again. He grabbed his long-distance communicator and pressed down the single button. 'Vey?' he spoke into it, loudly and clearly.

'Thordric?' Vey's voice came back out of it. The blue flower poking out of the top bobbed about from the vibrations. 'Having trouble already? We've only been gone a few hours,' he joked, but Thordric cut across him.

'Vey, I need your help. Kal had a mishap with one of his potions and now he's got craters all over his hands. I've given him some pain reducing potion, but I don't know what else to do.'

'Hmm,' Vey said. 'Up in my chambers you should find a bottle of what looks like liquid silver. Try putting it on each of the craters. It should speed up the skin growth in those areas. Be careful though, I haven't quite finished testing it yet.'

Thordric thanked him and took Kal up to Vey's room. It was back to how it usually looked now, with Vey's large wooden bed in the middle and his desk opposite. The room was circular, with bookshelves lining it entirely. Thordric scanned Vey's desk and saw the potion he'd told him about. He picked it up and looked at the label. Vey had written 'Super Cells' on it with his small, hasty writing.

'Come here, Kal,' he said over his shoulder, as Kal was trying to prise a large book off one of the shelves, trying not to use his hands too much.

Kal straightened, pushing the book back in place, and hurried over to where Thordric was standing. Thordric unscrewed the bottle and held it over Kal's hands. The orange potion was all gone now, absorbed quickly by Kal's skin. The craters looked less raw, but they were still deep. Carefully, Thordric poured one drop of the silver potion on each crater. 'Here it goes,' he said, as they watched it pool apprehensively.

3

THEY'RE GOING TO HAVE TO COME OFF!

The potion hissed slightly as Thordric and Kal waited for it to work. The silver colour really did make it resemble liquid metal, meaning Kal's hands looked like they'd been decorated with metal studs. However, after a few minutes, the hissing died down and the metal studs began to shrink away as the craters filled with freshly grown skin. Kal sighed, but Thordric was holding his breath – Vey hadn't finished testing the potion yet.

Kal's hands were almost back to normal now...but as Thordric had been suspecting, the skin kept growing.

'Thordric, what's happening?' Kal said, flicking his hands in the hope that it would stop. Unfortunately, it only made it worse. Now, instead of craters on his hands, he had great bobbles of skin. One moment they were pea-sized, then the next they were as big as walnuts.

'Uhhh...' said Thordric, putting the potion bottle down and searching Vey's desk frantically, looking to see if he had any notes on how to stop it. But there was nothing. He searched through all of the drawers, including several hidden ones he wasn't supposed to know about, and then all the bookshelves lined around the room. There had to be something.

Suddenly, Kal lunged at Thordric and grabbed at the pockets of his robes. He pulled out the long-distance communicator and, with extreme difficulty now that the lumps on his hands were each the size of a small plum, he pressed the button and half-screamed, half bellowed into it.

'High Wizard Vey! Your reverence, please help me!'

A loud spluttering sound came from the communicator and a good deal of coughing, as though Vey had choked on his tea. 'Is that you, Kal?' his voice came, sounding slightly weak.

'My hands, your reverence! I've got great balls of skin growing on them!' Kal shouted. He had gone completely white, and his hand shook while he held the communicator, making the small blue flower poking out of the top wobble unhappily.

There was a pause, in which Thordric was sure he heard Vey muttering a few curse words. 'I thought this could happen. Thordric, are you there?' he asked.

Thordric took the communicator from Kal. 'Yes, I'm here, Vey,' he said, trying to stay calm in order to set a good example. It was difficult, though, as his stomach had decided to do loop the loops right up to his chest.

'How big are the balls of skin on Kal's hands now?' Vey asked.

Thordric took a good look. 'They're almost apple sized. It looks as though they're all growing into each other. I don't think they're slowing down at all.'

They heard Vey take a deep breath. 'Right, there's nothing for it, Thordric. You have to take him to your mother's. She should be able to dispose of the excess skin. But first, you have to stop the growth.'

'How?' Thordric asked, wondering if it was even possible.

'This growth was potion induced, not by a spell. Surely the only way to stop it is by using another potion?'

'Not if you're determined,' Vey replied confidently. 'I know full well how good you are at stopping spell-induced growth. Remember the times when you fixed my uncle's moustache after your sisters pulled it out when they were babies?'

'Of course I do,' Thordric said, smirking at the memory in spite of the situation.

'Well, the same theory applies to this. Spell magic can override potions if you try hard enough.'

'Alright,' breathed Thordric. 'I'll try it.'

He took Kal's hands in his own. They felt a bit like knobbly playing balls, but he pushed the thought from his mind. Now was the time to concentrate. Slowing his breathing, he pushed his mind out to Kal's hands, trying to sense the duplication of the skin cells. It took him a while, but he found it. Now all he had to do was persuade them to stop.

It wasn't easy. Vey's silver potion was strong, and though he tried to push past it and break it up, it kept pushing his magic back. He began to sweat.

Kal, thankfully, was remaining silent. He'd seen Thordric work before and knew that he could do it, as long as he wasn't interrupted.

But Thordric was getting angry now. Forming a mental battering ram, he knocked against the stubborn wall of magic that the potion was putting up, willing with every ounce of power he had for it to work.

Then the potion's magic shattered, allowing him to get a firm grasp on the skin cells that were duplicating. Energy was pouring out of them like boiling hot waves. If he could reverse those waves, then the growth would stop.

Grasping at them with his mind, he tugged backwards. The wave reversed, but only slightly. He tugged again, harder, and then several more times. With each tug, the wave reversed even more, until it became so soft it was barely there. Thordric tugged one last time, and the wave stopped completely.

Kal looked at his hands. 'Thordric, you did it!' he said excitably, shaking them about and accidentally hitting Thordric full on the nose with a thud, knocking him to the floor.

'Perhaps I should take you to my mother's now,' Thordric said dizzily, his eyes glazed.

Maggie, Thordric's mother, was wearing a long, velvet dressing gown when she answered the door. She stared at them, but then spotted Kal's hands and let out a small cry of excitement, ushering them inside.

As she led them into the lounge, they saw the inspector sitting in an armchair, deeply immersed in an article of the Jard Town Gazette. Thordric peered over his shoulder. It was an article in the health section, on the management of moustache hair loss. Thordric fought to suppress his snigger, but the inspector noticed him and jumped up in fright.

'For Spell's sake, boy, don't startle me like that,' he said, his own moustache fraying slightly.

'Sorry, Inspector,' Thordric said, grinning. He still hadn't been able to shake the habit of calling him that, despite the fact that the inspector had been married to his mother for six years now. 'But you were so busy reading that I didn't want to disturb you.'

The inspector glared at him. 'What are you doing here at this time of night, anyway?'

Thordric looked a little guilty, glancing over to where Kal was now in deep discussion with Maggie. He had a very pained look on his face. 'Well, my student, Kal, had an accident with some anti-acne potion he was brewing, and when I tried to fix things with a potion that Vey suggested, it didn't quite work out the way we'd hoped.'

'A potion that my esteemed nephew suggested? He gave you the wrong advice, then?' the inspector asked, a rather nasty gleam in his eyes.

'I didn't say that,' Thordric protested. 'Vey warned us that the potion might not be ready, but he's away at the moment and could only advise us on the long-distance communicator.'

'Hmm. Well, I suppose he couldn't help it then,' the inspector said, the gleam fading. The inspector got on fairly well with Vey, but he always seemed to relish in other people's mistakes. Thordric'd had personal experience of his delight many times; far too many to count, in fact.

The inspector coughed, changing the subject. 'I see you've recovered from your fainting spell the other day. I don't think I've seen anyone change from one colour to another so quickly. First you went pink, then slightly green, and finally grey, before landing on the floor.'

Thordric tried hard not to remember. How could he have fainted in front of a room full of senior wizards like that, even if they were all friends of his? Thankfully, the only person who seemed to have taken any glee from it was Wizard Ayek, who everyone knew was a stubborn git so stuck in the past that he couldn't even tell what day of the week it was. The only reason why Vey hadn't asked him to leave the council was because he knew there was nowhere for him to go; Ayek had lived at the council for over forty years.

'It's no good, Thordric,' his mother called over to him. Kal was looking at him too, ghostly white and shaking so much that his short dreadlocks rocked about like pendulums.

'What do you mean?' Thordric asked, looking from her to Kal.

'They're going to have to come off.'

'WHAT?' he said, his eyes widening in horror.

His mother put her finger to her lips and shushed him. 'The twins are asleep upstairs. If you wake them up now, then they'll never go back to sleep.'

Thordric made a mental effort to calm himself. 'What do you mean, they have to come off?' he whispered, indicating Kal's hands.

'I've got to cut off the extra lumps of skin. There's no other way of getting rid of it,' she said, sighing.

Thordric sighed too. 'Oh, I thought you meant that you had to cut off his hands,' he said.

'Well,' his mother said archly, 'I suppose I *could* do that. After all, wizards can still use magic without their hands, can't they?'

Kal let out a whimper. Thordric's mother laughed. 'Don't worry, Kal, just because the morgue has been empty lately doesn't mean I'm suffering from enough withdrawal to start amputating hands unnecessarily.' Then she looked at Thordric seriously. 'It will hurt him though, and I don't have any anaesthetic here to dull the pain. Have you got any potions on you that do something similar?'

Thordric frowned and searched his pockets, but they were empty. 'We've got some in the stock cupboard at the council; I saw the bottle this morning while I was looking for ingredients. As long as no one has moved it, I should be able to summon it here.'

His mother gave an approving nod, making her thick, curly brown hair bounce about her shoulders. Thordric went over to the table and sat down. He closed his eyes, picturing the bottle of lime green potion which stood on the third shelf in the council's stock cupboard. He could see the chips on the glass where someone had carelessly knocked it against another bottle many times before.

He opened his eyes, still seeing the bottle clearly, and willed it to appear on the table in front of him. Within moments, the bottle appeared with a soft clunk. He picked it up and gave it to his mother. 'That's the strongest numbing potion that we've got. Spread it thinly all over his hands, but be careful not to touch it yourself, otherwise you'll go numb too.'

An hour later, with his hands bandaged up once more and with no sign of any craters or lumps on them, Kal returned to his room at the Training Facility escorted by Thordric.

He'd sworn never to try any advanced potions like that again unless Thordric was there to help him and was under strict orders from Maggie not to use his hands much over the next few days until they healed a bit.

As Thordric made his way to his own room, greeting a group of wizards who had been doing some late-night research along the way, he wished that Vey would hurry up and come back. He felt so unsure without the High Wizard around, even though he knew it was only for a few days.

Though Vey was in his early forties, he was the closest thing to a brother that Thordric had ever had, and, more often than not, acted like his father as well.

It was strange; Thordric had never known his father, and his mother refused to speak about him other than to mention that he had been a full wizard, yet he couldn't help wondering what his life would have been like if he'd have known him.

He got into bed, punching his pillow into shape until it was comfortable, before dropping off into a fitful, dream-laden sleep.

Despite Thordric's initial worry, the next three days without Vey passed by without incident. The Wizard Council went about its business as usual and, only when Vey's mother,

Lizzie, turned up, demanding to know where he'd gone and why no one had thought to tell her (she'd found out from her brother, the inspector), did he feel remotely stressed.

Indeed, once he'd calmed Lizzie down with the council's special blend of tea, he had a fun time showing her around the building. She had never seen the inside before, despite wanting to visit the moment Vey had opened it up for the public. It sounded like that he'd come up with every possible excuse for her not to come, but she'd been determined this time and Thordric, who she'd initially trained, liked her company.

Of course, many of the other wizards found it unnerving to have a woman walking around who had a deep understanding of magic, for like every other woman in the country, she had no magic herself. Of course, what most of the wizards at the council didn't know was that her husband had been a half-wizard, and over the years that he'd spent harnessing and learning how to use his own magic, she had watched him closely and observed all the techniques he'd tried. Therefore, her knowledge on the subject was equal to (or greater, as Thordric suspected) their own, and she took great pleasure in having long, rather loud discussions about it with Thordric.

Kal had kept out of sight for the duration of her visit; he was terrified of her due to Thordric's slightly elaborated tales of when she'd first trained him. The very mention of her name was enough to send the young wizard running to the other side of the building.

After Lizzie had gone home and evening was drawing in, Thordric busied himself with preparing everything for Vey's return the next day. It involved arranging an alarming amount of paperwork, and as he was sorting it into piles according to what the subject was, Kal once again knocked hard on the door.

Before Thordric could open it, the young wizard barged

into the room, narrowly missing Thordric's face with the door handle.

He was breathless, his dreadlocks were swinging around wildly, and his brow was wet with sweat. 'It's Hamlet,' he managed, his lips shaking. 'He's back, but...'

Thordric got to his feet at once. 'Take me to him,' he said. Kal didn't need telling twice. He sprinted out of the room and down the twisting halls, not even looking to see if Thordric was behind him.

Hamlet was in the entrance hall, completely soaked from the rain outside. He was covered in scratches and grazes, and when he saw Thordric, he started babbling incoherently.

Thordric grabbed him by the shoulders and held him still. 'Hamlet, calm down. Breathe, and tell me what happened.'

'H-h-h-h-high Wizard Vey is...is...'

But that was all Thordric could get out of him before Hamlet collapsed on the floor, his eyes staring blankly up at the ceiling.

4

A STRANGER APPEARS

'Hamlet?' Thordric said, shaking his blond friend gently by the shoulders.

He and Kal had taken Hamlet to Lizzie's house so that the other wizards wouldn't panic about whatever it was he had to say, and while Hamlet was still unconscious, Thordric had tried to reach Vey on his long-distance communicator to see if he was alright. There had been no reply; Thordric couldn't even make out any background noises to suggest where Vey was.

Lizzie came in from the kitchen with a tray of tea and cakes. 'Is he awake yet?' she asked quietly, placing the tray down on the coffee table.

As she did so, Hamlet stirred. They had put him on the same sofa that Thordric had been lying on when he'd fainted, and as Hamlet opened his eyes, he panicked and promptly fell off onto the floor. Thordric and Kal picked him up, holding him steady, as it appeared as though his legs didn't want to work. Hamlet looked at them, his eyes taking a while to focus.

'Thordric? Where am I?' he asked, his voice quivering.

'We've brought you to Lizzie's. We thought it would be calmer here,' Thordric replied.

'Oh,' Hamlet said, but then he jumped up again. 'High Wizard Vey! I must tell you about him! You have to come quickly, there's no time for a carriage. He's...it's...we've got to go, we've got to leave now!' He made to run for the door, but Kal and Thordric held him back.

'Calm down, Hamlet, and drink some of this,' Lizzie said firmly, pressing down on Hamlet's shoulder so that he sat back down. She held a large mug of the council's most effective calming tea out to him. He struggled against it at first, but they held his head still and poured it down his throat. After a minute, he relaxed enough for them to let go.

'Now, start slowly and tell us everything,' Lizzie told him, in a voice that no one could argue with.

Hamlet took a long, deep breath before speaking barely louder than a whisper. 'High Wizard Vey and I left for the forest that I told Thordric about before. I think it's called Teroosa Forest; it's not far from here, about a day's ride by carriage if you leave at dawn. Of course, we left in the evening and decided to camp outside overnight—'

Kal choked at this. 'You let the High Wizard sleep *outside*? What if you'd been ambushed or something?'

Hamlet shook his head slightly. 'High Wizard Vey put up a shield while we slept. Nothing could have gotten through unless he allowed it. Of course, it did make it difficult when I had to get up for a call of nature during the night...' His cheeks flushed as he realised what he'd said, but the others took no notice.

'When we got into Teroosa Forest, late the following afternoon, we went down the pathway to the statues I found there. When the High Wizard saw them, he went white and told me they weren't statues at all, they were people who'd been frozen in time. Apparently, it's a form of magic that he's only come across recently through reading one of Kalljard's early journals. He said it's deep, powerful magic that takes more skill than any other spell he knows of.'

He took another breath but didn't speak. Instead, he drained the rest of the tea they had given him.

'But then what happened?' Thordric asked, studying his friend.

'I...I don't know exactly. One moment High Wizard Vey was standing in front of both statues, and then...then...'

At that moment, there was a knock on Lizzie's front door. She swept out of the room to answer it but gave a cry of alarm. Before the others could get up, a man in his late twenties strode in, resembling a slightly older version of Thordric.

'Sorry to disturb you,' he said, his voice sounding like he hadn't used it in years. 'But I wonder if you could help me?'

The words were no sooner out of his mouth, however, than Hamlet saw him and jumped to his feet, pointing. 'You!' he said, staring at the man in sheer horror. 'You...'

The man gaped back at him, obviously having no idea who Hamlet was. By this time, Lizzie had come back into the room, looking slightly pale, but down to business as usual.

'You recognise this man, Hamlet?' she asked, her eyebrow arching.

Hamlet swallowed. 'He...was one of the statues. When High Wizard Vey stood in front of him and the other one, something happened and suddenly he became a man again. But the High Wizard was still concentrating, and suddenly *he* turned into a statue instead.'

'Vey's a statue?' Thordric cried.

'I was a statue?' the stranger said, wonderingly.

'Yes, and yes,' Hamlet said rapidly. 'That's what I've been trying to tell you.'

Thordric's legs gave way and he had to sit down, nursing his head. 'But how...?'

'I don't know,' Hamlet replied, 'but if anyone can help him, it's *you*.'

Thordric started shaking. What could possibly have happened for Vey to have been turned into a statue? He was capable of warding off even the strongest of magics, how could he get caught out by something like this?

He turned to the strange man. 'Who are you?' he asked.

The man looked at him, and around at everyone else. 'I can't remember,' he said. 'All I know is that for some reason, I knew the way to this house. And I know you,' he continued, staring at Lizzie. 'Though you seem to have aged since then.'

'Indeed. It was over many years ago when Patrick, my husband, was still alive. He was researching various plants for their potion making qualities.' She looked at Thordric. 'Do you remember all those maps of forests we found at my country house?'

Thordric thought for a moment. It'd been when she had taken him there for a week of full-on training before he'd joined the council. He had wanted to find a plan of the house, but as they were searching for it, they came across a bundle of maps all depicting different forests. He recalled that there *was* one labelled Teroosa Forest.

'Yes, I remember,' he said, after a pause.

'Well, one day after visiting one of those forests, Patrick came back with someone; a young man who seemed to have lost his memory. Patrick explained that he'd broken a spell on the man, one that he'd been under for so long he had no idea who he was or where he was from. The young man stayed with us for a few months and slowly regained some of his memories, enough to tell us his name was Ourellus and that he was a wizard. Patrick helped him re-learn how to use his magic, though it was still patchy. Then one day he disappeared...until now.'

She looked hard at the man, but he stared back at her blankly. 'You say...my name was Ourellus?' he breathed.

She nodded. 'I can't be certain, but it sounds as though someone put you back under the spell Patrick released you from, but now my son, High Wizard Vey, has set you free once more. He probably recognized you from when he was a teenager.'

Thordric, Kal and Hamlet eyed them both, trying to take in everything Lizzie had said.

'But who would put someone under a spell like that, for all this time?' Kal asked, but Thordric already knew the answer.

'There's only one person I know who would have been strong enough and knowledgeable enough to do something like that. Kalljard.'

'My father?' Kal said, though he wasn't as surprised as he made out to be. No one was sure if he was really Kalljard's son, but there had been rumours around that Kalljard had fathered a boy. Either way, his mother had believed it was true enough to keep him hidden from Kalljard when he was alive, for had Kalljard known, he would have killed Kal along with all the other half-wizards he'd planned to eradicate.

'The only thing that's bothering me is *why* Kalljard would do it. What could Ourellus have done to make Kalljard freeze him in time?' Thordric said.

'I only wish I could remember. Perhaps if I go back to the forest something will come back to me,' Ourellus answered.

'Well, we've got to go there for Vey,' Thordric said. 'I hope my magic's strong enough to help him. Though if it's a spell of Kalljard's, I'm not so sure.'

'Was this Kalljard really so powerful?' Ourellus asked, though at the looks he received, he knew the answer was yes.

'Kalljard built this town about a thousand years ago and formed the Wizard Council. Before that, wizards worked on their own, doing whatever they felt necessary. It didn't matter whether they were full wizards or half-wizards; as long as they had magic, they used it to help people. After Kalljard formed the council, however, everything changed. He remained High Wizard until he died six years ago,' Thordric explained.

'That's an awfully long time to be alive,' Ourellus said, frowning. 'How did he do it?'

'Well, we knew he took a potion that stopped him from ageing, but after he died, we analysed the ingredients, and I don't believe it was powerful enough to prolong his life by itself. The extent of his powers is still a mystery, something that we might not ever find out,' Thordric continued.

'But we have more pressing matters to discuss for now,' Lizzie said, stepping forwards. 'What is going to happen to the council with my poor Eric in such a state?'

Ourellus looked at her, puzzled. 'Eric is Vey's real name,' Thordric explained.

'She's right, Thordric,' Kal pointed out. 'If you go searching for Vey, then the council will have no one in charge.'

Thordric frowned, but then peered at Lizzie, a mysterious grin on his face. 'Oh, yes they will.'

'Come now, boy, are you sure this is a good idea?' Lizzie said as Thordric led her down the halls to the council's meeting room.

He had called an emergency gathering the moment they all arrived back at the council, and as they walked into the room, a sea of wizards looked up at him with a mix of curiosity and apprehension on their faces. It was almost dawn now, and most of them were still in their nightclothes. Thordric resisted a smirk as he saw that Wizard Ayek favoured nightclothes of a vibrant pink.

'Of course it's a good idea,' Thordric replied happily, still grinning foolishly at his own brilliance. He took his place at the head of the room, ignoring the suspicious whispers as the wizards all eyed Lizzie.

He cleared his throat loudly. 'Wizards of the council, I fear I must tell you that I bring grave news. High Wizard Vey has been trapped within a spell that has turned him into a statue. It seems it's a type of ancient magic known as being frozen in time.'

There was complete silence while his words sank in. Then the hall erupted in cries of horror and anger, growing into a babble so loud that Thordric could only hear snatches of what the wizards were saying.

'—just *knew* something like this would happen—'

'—the High Wizard, trapped? How—'

'—and time magic? Ridiculous—'

Eventually, Thordric held up his hands to quiet them down. It took several minutes before they were ready to listen again, and only then did they stop because he made all the fireplaces pop at the same time.

'Do you have a plan, Thordric?' a wizard named Batsu, who was fifteen years older than Thordric and one of his closest friends, asked.

'Yes, I do have a plan. After speaking with Hamlet, who was with High Wizard Vey at the time this incident occurred, I have decided to travel to the forest where the High Wizard is and try to free him. Whether I will succeed, I do not know, for our theory is that the spell has something to do with Kalljard.'

'Kalljard?' Wizard Ayek piped up. 'But he's dead. How can he cast a spell if he's dead?'

A vein in Thordric's temple began to throb as he looked at

the man. 'I do not know, but I assure you it is my intention to find out.'

'But why should you go? Shouldn't we send someone with more experience?' Wizard Ayek pressed, sneering slightly.

'And who here has more experience with dangerous magic than Thordric?' Wizard Batsu shot back at him. 'You certainly don't.'

'Why you—'

'Enough,' Lizzie said, taking stage, even more irritated than Thordric was. 'High Wizard Vey is my son, and I deem Thordric fit to undertake this task. If you want to argue the matter, then do it with me.'

The hall was silent once more. Thordric knew it had been a good idea to bring her.

'Lizzie's right, we have no time to argue the matter. Myself, Hamlet, and Kal shall leave for Teroosa Forest within the hour—'

'You're letting Kal go with you? What if he accidentally blows High Wizard Vey to bits? What will you do then?' Ayek spat.

Lizzie gave him a withering look that made him shut his mouth immediately.

'Before we leave, however,' Thordric continued, 'there is something I need to take care of. With both myself and High Wizard Vey gone, there is no one to take the head of the council. I suggest that Lady Elizabeth, High Wizard Vey's mother, be given charge.'

The hall gaped at him, including Lizzie herself.

'But she's a woman. Women don't have any magic; we can't let someone without magic head the Wizard Council, even if she is the High Wizard's mother,' Ayek said, and this time there was a loud murmur of agreement.

'How are you going to get around that one, boy?' Lizzie

34

asked Thordric, moving only the corner of her mouth. But Thordric winked at her.

'Lady Elizabeth has great knowledge of magic, even if she does not possess it herself, and she has a sound mind for matters of organisation and reason. The day to day running of the council will be a task she can do with ease, I assure you. If, however, a situation does arise that demands the need for serious magic, then I trust you all to work together to assist her to the best of your abilities.'

There was some spluttering from the crowd, but Lizzie, impressed by Thordric's speech, said, 'You heard the boy. I will step in as head of the council for as long as it takes for my son to be revived. I expect no arguments on this matter, and if anyone sees fit to do so, I believe there are some suitable punishments available.'

Even Thordric stepped back at this. When Lizzie was serious, she could be awfully intimidating.

5

FROZEN IN TIME

The carriage bumped its way down the narrow lane leading out from the back of the Wizard Council to the streets of Jard Town. Thordric and Hamlet started suffering from travel sickness almost as soon as the carriage had started moving, but luckily Thordric had filled his pockets with vials of anti-sickness potion. After drinking a whole vial each, their stomachs appeared to settle down enough so that they could get some sleep like Kal and Ourellus, both of whom had already started snoring.

Thordric had thought about stopping off at Lizzie's house near Watchem Woods to get her husband's map of Teroosa Forest, but that was in the opposite direction to where they were headed, and he didn't want to delay getting to Vey any more than they had already. Instead, though he'd been doubtful of doing so, as the last time he'd seen the map was six years ago, he had managed to summon it just before they headed out. Lizzie had helped him, describing its exact location in the house.

Feeling much better now that the potion was taking effect,

Thordric found he was too awake to attempt sleep yet. Trying not to disturb the others, he pulled the map out of Hamlet's over-filled bag and studied it. The forest was large; there were several lakes spread though out the trees and, drawn in fine pencil rather than the pen that had been used for the rest of the details, was a small depiction of a statue. He wasn't surprised that he hadn't seen it before, because it was so faded, he could barely make out enough of it to trace with his finger. He looked closer and saw that there was another one right next to it.

So, Patrick, Lizzie's husband, *had* really seen the statues that Hamlet and Vey had gone to study. He glanced across at Ourellus, who was now slouched over to the side, dribbling slightly from the corner of his mouth. Had he really been one of them?

They had given Ourellus a few drops of potion that was still in development, which was supposed to help people with amnesia regain their memories, but so far, he couldn't remember anything more than what Lizzie had revealed to them all. He had, however, demonstrated that his magic was perfectly fine. In fact, Thordric had to admit that he seemed almost as strong as Vey. Perhaps that was why Kalljard had frozen him in time; he might have seen him as a threat. He knew for certain that while Kalljard had been alive, Vey had deliberately hidden much of his ability in order to avoid that very situation. Of course, now that Vey was High Wizard he could (and indeed was encouraged to by the public, for they liked nothing more than to see powerful magic demonstrated skilfully) use his abilities freely.

Thordric yawned and tucked the map back into Hamlet's bag. The journey would take the rest of the day and, as he had no way of knowing what the situation would be like in the forest, he decided not to think about it and pulled out his notebook instead. Maybe he would find a way to make his dish-washing spell work while he was travelling.

Thordric felt a rough shaking on his shoulders and opened his eyes to see that the sky was inky black outside the carriage. He looked around; Kal was leaning over him, checking to see if he was awake. Only then did Thordric realise that the carriage had stopped. He could hear Ourellus and Hamlet already outside, unloading their bags.

'We're here, Thordric,' Kal said, picking up the notebook that had slid off Thordric's lap as he'd slept and giving it to him.

Thordric stretched his neck, rubbing the sleep from his eyes. He stepped out into the night, pulling his cloak tighter as the chill night air bit into him. He tried to look into the distance, but it was far too dark to make anything out. He felt a tap on his shoulder and turned around. Hamlet was standing behind him, holding out a large, round globe. Thordric took it and shook it vigorously; the potion inside the globe reacted instantly, lighting up the area around them. These light globes had been an invention of Lizzie's husband's, and ever since he'd found out about them, Thordric had kept a few handy.

Hamlet handed them out to the others, and soon they had enough light to see the path that led into the forest. Thordric tipped the carriage driver, who thanked him and wished them a safe excursion before pulling away into the darkness.

'It's up to you, Hamlet,' Thordric said. 'Show us the way.'

Hamlet nodded and took the lead, though the light of his globe shook slightly as he shivered up the path. He led them to the right as soon as they'd gone through the first lot of trees, and after about ten minutes, headed left towards the centre of the forest. As far as Thordric remembered, it appeared as though

Hamlet was taking them towards the place marked on the map, but his sense of direction was so bad he couldn't be sure.

'I thought you said you only explored a little bit before you found them before,' Thordric said to Hamlet after they'd been walking for two hours.

Hamlet grinned sheepishly. 'Well, it *was* just a little bit of exploring to me. If I had explored the forest properly, then I wouldn't have been back for another month. It's strange, though; before I came across it, I had no idea that this forest was here, and I've studied maps of Dinia more times than I can count.'

Ourellus laughed. 'That's probably because my mother didn't want you to know about it,' he said.

They all looked at him. 'Your mother?' Kal asked him curiously. 'Have you got your memory back then?'

Ourellus blinked, his face as puzzled as everyone else's. 'No...I...I'm not sure why I said that.' He shrugged and they carried on walking. Thordric frowned at him, his eyes boring into Ourellus's back. In the globe's light, they looked even more like each other than before. They even had the same bald spot on their chins where hair absolutely refused to grow.

Suddenly, Ourellus turned around and caught Thordric staring. 'Is something the matter?' he asked, a note of irritation in his voice.

Thordric coughed awkwardly. 'No, it's nothing. Never mind,' he said, and sped up so that he caught up with Hamlet. 'You know, Hamlet, I'm always finding places that I've overlooked. The other day, I found a passageway at the council that I'd never been down before, but I must have walked past the entrance every day.'

Kal snorted. 'I remember that. You got stuck in there and had to call me for help. It took Vey to get you out, because one of Kalljard's spells was on it that made trespassers too broad shouldered to get through.'

'You didn't have to mention that part,' Thordric sniffed. 'But you see, it's easy not to spot things when you're not looking for them.'

Hamlet smiled. 'Did you ever find out what was down there?' he asked, his eyes alight with curiosity.

'Yes, actually. After Vey managed to get me out, we both took a crack at breaking the spell, and after we'd done it, we followed the passageway all the way through. It came out into a room that must have been at least two floors underground. It was full of Kalljard's stuff; that's probably where Vey found Kalljard's notes on this frozen in time spell. I wish I knew where he put them; they might have told me how to reverse it.'

As he finished speaking, he realised that Hamlet had stopped, holding up his light globe and indicating for the others to do the same. The light hit the trees around them, illuminating two statues a few feet away. Hamlet was right; they did look like they'd been carved out of crystal.

Thordric moved closer, holding up his light globe so that he could see their features more clearly. The one closest to him was a woman, slight of figure but with a challenging look about her face. She had long hair, down to her ankles, which was floating out behind her as if she had been caught in the wind. He turned to the other one, a tall man dressed in long robes, with shoulder-length hair and a goatee style beard. It was Vey.

His eyes had been frozen open, a look of deep surprise on his face, and he had his hands up as though trying to ward something off. Thordric analysed him closely and noticed the long-distance communicator sticking out of his pocket. So that's why they hadn't been able to contact him.

'So, what do we do now?' Kal asked soberly.

'I suppose I should try and break the spell. If I can get a

grasp on what the spell's components are to create that effect, then maybe I can—'

'No! You mustn't do that,' Ourellus said sharply. 'It's too dangerous. The spell that binds him was one of my brother's trap spells. If you attempt to remove it, then it will simply transfer itself to you.'

Thordric turned to him. Ourellus was looking at him seriously, without a trace of the confusion that had hung over him since they'd met. 'Your...brother's spell? Are you trying to tell us that Kalljard...was your brother?' he said in disbelief.

'Yes. I remember everything now; coming to this forest must have freed my mind.' He took a deep breath, acknowledging their urge for an explanation. 'When Kalljard and I were boys, we were very competitive with each other, but he was always stronger than me despite the fact that he was born barely alive. When he got older and got it into his head that all wizards should group together and become the Wizard Council, I, and my mother, tried to talk him out of it. You see, his thirst for domination had already become apparent and his dislike for other half-wizards was growing stronger by the day. My mother and I both knew that if things went his way, many people would suffer—'

'*Other* half-wizards?' Thordric choked. 'You mean that Kalljard was one?'

'Of course he was. Our father was a wizard, and both Kalljard and myself were born with magic. Under those circumstances, how could he not have been?' Ourellus replied simply, clearly amused at Thordric's reaction. 'Anyway, despite our protests, Kalljard decided to go ahead with his plans, but mother tried to use her magic against him and he punished her for it. She was frozen first, with three different spells; one to seal her magic, one to freeze her, and one to act as a trap should I get it into my head to free her. For a while, I didn't dare attempt anything against him, but when he moved to where Jard Town now stands and used his magic to drive out all the tribes living there so that he could claim the land for his own, I lost my temper. I made a deal with the tribes to use my magic to help them fight against him, but he caught wind of my plan and froze me too.'

He took a breath and cleared his throat. 'How it happened, I don't know, but one day I woke from my frozen state at the hands of a half-wizard called Patrick. He took me back to his house and he and his wife helped me recover. After a while, however, I regained enough of my memory to remember who Kalljard was and what he had done and set off to see what he was up to. I knew by then that he'd successfully formed the Wizard Council, and I saw there were no traces of the old tribes left in the town. In my anger, I found a group of wizards and demanded that they take me to him. They took me for insane and used defensive spells on me. One of them knocked me over in front of an oncoming carriage, but a young woman who was walking by saw and pushed me out of the way before it could hit me.'

His cheeks went slightly pink at this point, and his voice grew softer. 'I'm afraid to say that I got distracted at that point and fell head over heels for her. We were married a month later, but barely two weeks had passed when Kalljard heard of my whereabouts. He kidnapped me while my wife was out and froze me again. Obviously, the spells he put on me were not as strong as those he put on my mother, for again someone has managed to free me.'

Thordric swallowed. 'So...when you mentioned your mother, did you mean...?' he gestured to the statue of the woman, who looked far too young to be anyone's mother, let alone a man in his mid-twenties. Though, he supposed that if Ourellus was telling the truth, he must be far older than that.

They all gathered around the woman. 'Yes,' said Ourellus, gazing at her. 'This is my mother.'

'Fascinating as all this is,' Kal broke in, 'I still don't see how this helps us free Vey.'

Hamlet and Thordric looked at him. He was right, none of this information helped them in the slightest.

'Mother may know. She's the one who knew Kalljard's magic best,' Ourellus said.

'But I thought you just told Thordric it was too dangerous for him to break the spell?' Hamlet pointed out.

'No, I said not to try and break the spell on Vey,' Ourellus clarified. 'If I'm right, Vey tried to lift the spells on mother entirely, but as soon as he attempted it, the trap spell froze him. Which means,' he added, rolling his eyes at the blank expression on their faces, 'that the only spells left on her are the one sealing her magic and the one keeping her frozen. It should be completely safe to lift it.'

Thordric raised his eyebrow doubtfully. 'Well, if you feel like trying it, go ahead,' he said.

Ourellus looked pained. 'I'm afraid I'm too out of practice to try and use my magic. It's going to have to be you or Kal.'

Kal was pleased that Ourellus had considered him able to do it, but as he stepped forwards to try, Hamlet and Thordric grabbed him by the shoulders and pulled him back.

'Hey!' he complained, but they ignored him.

'Stay back, then,' Thordric said, leaving Kal to Hamlet. 'I don't know what's going to happen, so be ready to run if things look bad.'

He gulped, trying to focus his mind.

Reaching out his consciousness towards the statue, he felt a hum around him. He pulled his mind back and then, attentively, put his hand on the statue's crystal-like surface. It was pulsing, like a heartbeat. He drew his hand back quickly, suddenly understanding. The frozen in time spell was already very weak; Vey must have seen to that. All Thordric had to do was pull the last remnants off and Ourellus's mother would be freed.

He took a breath and reached out with his consciousness again, searching for the edges of the spell with his mind. The humming grew louder in his ears until it was almost unbearable. He had found it. Taking another deep breath, he pulled at the spell. It tore easily, and the young woman fell to the floor by his feet.

6

LYANIS

Ourellus rushed forwards and helped her up, taking her over to a fallen tree and letting her rest against it. Then he took a flask of tea from their bags and poured her a cup. She took it gratefully, her hands shaking, and sipped it slowly.

As Thordric watched her, he saw her skin was not pale, tanned, or brown like most people's, but a silvery grey colour. He blinked, sure that it was just the light, but no matter which way he looked at her, her skin stayed the same.

Eventually her shaking subsided enough for her to raise her head, taking in all the faces staring at her. 'Ourellus...is it really you?' she asked, her voice low, yet somehow reminding Thordric of birdsong. It carried the same sort of strength that he'd noticed in her face while she'd been frozen.

But it wasn't Ourellus, who was sitting beside her, that she was addressing. It was Thordric. He gazed at her, bewildered. 'No,' he said. 'I'm Thordric. That's Ourellus there.' He pointed to Ourellus, whose face was stony as he glared at Thordric.

The young woman turned to Ourellus, her eyes narrowed closely as she studied him. 'Indeed, that is true,' she said. 'But you are older than I remember you. Tell me, what has happened? Is Kalljard still attempting to form his council and take over this land?'

There was silence as Ourellus stared awkwardly at his feet. Finally, it was Hamlet who spoke up. 'Kalljard formed the Wizard Council and Jard Town over a thousand years ago. He's been dead for six years now.'

It took a moment for this information to sink in, but when it did, she surprised them all by laughing for so long that the tension between everyone grew extremely uncomfortable. Eventually, she stopped, drinking some more tea.

'This drink is nice; I can taste the magic of the earth within it,' she said as she put the cup down. 'So, I've been frozen for a thousand years or so? I knew my son was strong, but I never dreamt that his magic would hold out that long. What has happened during that time? Tell me everything,' she asked, though her words had a curtness to them that made it more of a demand.

Between them, they all filled her in on the founding of Jard Town and the Wizard Council, the oppression of half-wizards and those, such as the Wanderers; a group of wizards who lived in Neathin Valley; who had never agreed with Kalljard's ways. Thordric then told her how Kalljard died; murdered by accident by High Wizard Vey, who, determined to try and change the council for the better, had tried to use a plant essence to make him hallucinate. Unfortunately, it reacted to the ingredients in Kalljard's life prolonging potion and ultimately killed him.

Ourellus told her his story too, from the point when he'd seen Kalljard freeze her to the moment when he had been frozen the second time and then freed by Vey. She looked at him, amused when he'd mentioned his marriage, but had made no comment. After they had all finished talking, she stood up, her legs unsteady at first, and walked around. She touched the ground here and there and ran her hands around Vey's frozen shoulders.

'Well, that would explain it, then,' she murmured to herself.

'Explain what?' asked Thordric, looking at Vey too. Before she could answer however, Kal popped out a question that he simply couldn't hold in anymore.

'What are you?' he asked, glancing around at Hamlet and Thordric, seeing they were also curious.

'Whatever do you mean...Kal, is it? Have you never seen a forest dweller before?' she said, staring around at them in complete surprise. He, Thordric and Hamlet all shook their heads. 'My, my, Kalljard has been busy,' she muttered in disgust.

'Forest dwellers are the protectors of forests like this one. They live until either the forest dies, or they wish to depart from life and leave the forest's care with another. We do not age as people do, for it is not in our interest to. Had I not foreseen what Kalljard would do to me, this forest would have died long ago. As it was, I managed to leave enough of my magic here to keep it alive for a time, long enough for my replacement to be born. However, it appears that she is still not ready, and the rest of my magic is sealed by the same spell on your friend over there,' she continued, nodding to Vey.

'So, it's true that you can use magic, even though you're a woman?' Kal asked in awe.

'Is that so very unusual, then?' she asked, her eyes growing large.

'Yes, only men have magic,' Thordric explained. 'I've always thought it was odd; it made things seem unbalanced somehow, but no women have had magic in all the recorded history of Dinia,' he continued, blushing as she looked at him.

47

She really was very pretty. It was difficult to think that she was Kalljard and Ourellus's mother.

Ourellus noticed. 'Mother, stop that,' he said curtly.

She turned to him and pouted. 'You always did object to my idea of fun,' she said, and Thordric realised how much he was staring and looked away. She laughed at him, gently this time, but then turned serious. 'I think I may know why the women of this age have all been born without magic. It is not that they lack it, but rather that it is sealed along with mine. Kalljard's spells always did become sloppy when he was in a rage, and he certainly was at the time he froze me. I believe that when he sealed my magic, he took it too far and unwittingly ended up sealing the magic of all women.'

'If we were to break the seal on yours, then their magic would return?' Thordric asked, thinking of his mother and Lizzie with magic. He quickly swept the idea from his mind. Those two didn't need magic, they were strong minded enough as it was.

'I believe so,' she said.

'I knew it!' Hamlet said excitedly. 'Didn't I tell you, Thordric? Didn't I? I knew my findings weren't wrong.'

'Oh?' she asked.

Hamlet grinned at her happily. 'Well, though there may not be any written records of women using magic, I've recently dug up rather a lot of artefacts that suggest quite the opposite. I've been telling Thordric for weeks.'

She smiled at him, making him blush as well, until she caught sight of Ourellus's face and stopped. 'I suppose we should get to work on freeing this High Wizard of yours,' she said. 'You were going to ask for my help on how to do it, weren't you?'

'Uh, yes, actually,' Thordric replied. 'Ourellus said that

whoever tries to break the spells on him will have them transferred to themselves instead.'

'Indeed, they would,' she agreed, 'if they only plan on using
human magic. But there are many magics of this world, and
when Kalljard was born weak and dying, I gathered these
magics in order to save him. That's why his spells are so strong,
and this one in particular is enormously powerful. Only
someone who has all these different magics within them can
hope to break it and remain unscathed.'

'I understand that, but where can we find these other types
of magic? Surely someone in Dinia would have come across
them by now if—'

'Oh, they aren't in Dinia.'

'Then where?' Hamlet asked her.

'Goodness, don't tell me Kalljard abolished geography as
well?' she muttered. 'There are four countries surrounding this
one, are there not?'

'Well, yes, I suppose. But the borders have been shut for
centuries. Only a few people can even name them now,'
Hamlet said, his face flushing pink at his lack of knowledge.

'In that case, let me tell you,' she replied. 'To the north lies
Fyoras. West across the mountains we have Numteqa. Uoo is
found to the east, and finally Wyotis sits to the south. All of
these lands have powerful magics, and it is these magics that I
gathered and sealed inside Kalljard as an infant. To free your
High Wizard, you must gather these magics yourselves and seal
them inside you. However,' she added, looking particularly at
Thordric's apprehensive face. 'Things have changed very much
since my time, and if, as you say, the borders really have been
shut for centuries, then these lands which were once so open
and friendly to all who lived in Dinia, may now be far less so.'

'So, once we've gathered these magics, we'll be more powerful?' Kal asked, his eyes sparkling.

The woman eyed him suspiciously. 'You are not, by any chance, related to Kalljard, are you?' she asked, a note of hardness in her voice.

Kal flinched. 'Yes...I'm his son,' he said. 'How did you know?'

'I recognised that same spark in your eyes as the one that burned in his. You ought to be careful; if you allow that hunger to take control of you, it may warp you the same way that it did him,' she said. 'To think that you are my grandson...it is a strange thought, I admit. But,' she added, glancing from Ourellus to Thordric, 'I do not think you are my only one.'

Thordric and Ourellus goggled at each other, sheer horror on both of their faces. 'You don't mean...?' Ourellus began. 'No, it's not possible.'

'Don't be ridiculous, Ourellus. You just told me yourself that you were married before Kalljard froze you again. Given what I heard, that would be at least twenty or so years ago. Tell me, Thordric, how old are you?' she asked.

Thordric felt faint, and his throat became awfully dry. 'I'm twenty-one,' he said.

Ourellus coughed, and said, rather weakly, 'Your mother isn't a doctor, by any chance, by the name of Maggie?'

'No, she's not,' Thordric said, but before Ourellus could sigh with relief, he continued, 'she's a pathologist. She wanted to be a practicing doctor, but then I came along, and she had to find work that allowed her to look after me at the same time. I spent a lot of time in the morgue growing up.'

He swallowed, mirroring the look of horror that had etched itself onto Ourellus's face. Then they both collapsed to the ground in a dead faint, parallel to each other. Hamlet and Kal stared at them, while Ourellus's mother allowed the corners of her mouth to twitch up. Thordric and Ourellus really *did* look alike.

. . .

Thordric awoke to find that Hamlet and Kal had set up tents and were talking to each other in low voices. His grandmother (though his insides squirmed at the thought) was watching over him and Ourellus, who had been covered in thick, warm blankets.

The sky was still dark, at least the part he could see through the great mass of branches overhead. Dawn was obviously some way off. He sat up and stretched, trying to ignore Ourellus beside him, who was letting out deep snores and dribbling from the corner of his mouth again.

'I'm sorry it was such a shock to you, Thordric,' his grandmother said softly.

Thordric held up his hands in objection. 'I would rather know than be ignorant. But I still find it hard to believe.' He smiled. 'What should I call you, anyway? Grandmother doesn't really feel appropriate, seeing as you look younger than I am.'

'I agree, grandmother *does* seem a bit much,' she said. 'You may call me Lyanis.'

'Lyanis? It's pretty, but I admit it sounds like a name for a plant,' he said, hoping it wouldn't offend her.

'You're a bright one, aren't you?' she said approvingly. 'It is the name of a plant; the plant that I grew from.'

'You're part plant?' he asked, incredulously.

'Of course,' she said. 'All forest dwellers grow from plants. My replacement, who is growing from my own magic, started as a plant that I felt was worthy and strong enough to hold my powers.'

'If you can...reproduce...that way,' he said, struggling to find the right words, 'then how did you end up having Ourellus and Kalljard?'

'My beginnings may have been that of a plant, but my heart

and my being are very much a woman's. I fell for a young man who lost his way in this forest. He was scared of me at first, after realising that I wasn't human, but after a while we became attached to each other. We were never married, for that is a human convention which I feel is unnecessary, but we lived together happily for many years. Ourellus was born first, strong and healthy, but while I was pregnant with Kalljard, a disease swept through this forest, and I used much of my magic to fight it. It left me very weak, a weakness that was passed onto him after he was born, and my instincts as a mother were to save him in any way I could. I didn't want him to die for my failings, but given his nature, perhaps I made the wrong decision.'

Thordric noticed that there was a terrible sadness in her eyes as she spoke. 'You couldn't have known what he would become as an adult. No one can predict the future like that,' he said.

'Thank you, Thordric,' she said, placing her silvery grey hand on his shoulder. 'It's been a long time since I've spoken about it, and I confess that it pains me more than I knew.'

'May I ask what happened to my grandfather?' he said softly.

She sighed at him. 'As the years went by, he aged as all humans do, and a year or so before Kalljard froze Ourellus and I, he became ridden with a disease that I simply couldn't cure him of. It was hard watching him grow older while I remained youthful, but we both accepted that we could never have a full life together. We cherished the time we had, and it consoled me somewhat knowing that Ourellus and Kalljard would live much longer than normal humans due to my blood. Still, they will never reach the age that I am. Even though Kalljard created the prolonged life potion you mentioned, it would not have worked forever.'

'So, if Ourellus has a longer lifespan than most people, then does that mean I will, too?' he asked, nervously. He wasn't sure whether he liked the idea or not.

'Possibly,' she said, 'but only time will tell. Though, if you don't keep an eye on Kal, his may be considerably shorter.'

'His magic's a bit unsteady still, but he's not that bad,' Thordric laughed, but Lyanis shook her head.

'That is not what I mean. You must have noticed it by now, having trained him for a few years,' she said.

'How did you—'

'He and Hamlet told me while you were sleeping. I've heard that you're quite talented. But still, Kal's hunger for more power will be his undoing if it is not kept under control. Neither I, nor you, I believe, would wish to see that happen.'

Thordric looked at her seriously. He knew she was right, for he'd sensed it within Kal before, not to mention that the incident in Neathin Valley had started because the young wizard had wanted to seek out more power to prove his magic was useful.

Ourellus snorted in his sleep and woke himself up, making them jump. He sat up, bleary eyed. His stomach groaned loudly, and he went rather red. 'I don't suppose we have any food, do we? I'm awfully hungry.'

Thordric stared at him, but his own stomach rumbled just as noisily, and he had to look away. Lyanis watched them and laughed. 'Like father, like son, I suppose,' she said cheerily, as Hamlet and Kal sniggered in the background before getting up to search their bags for food.

7

LIZZIE TAKES CHARGE

Thordric contacted Lizzie on his long-distance communicator as soon as the sun rose. After briefly explaining what the situation was, she immediately responded by sending Wizard Batsu to get them on the Wizard Council's small floating ship named *Dinia's Jewel*.

The ship was the fastest one in the country, as Vey had tweaked it when he'd first discovered it tucked away in the cargo hold of one of the larger Ships of Kal; huge floating vessels that carried people all over Dinia. As *Dinia's Jewel* was so fast, Batsu reached them only two hours after Thordric had sent word.

As he let down the rope ladder so that they could climb aboard, he called over to Thordric. 'Is it true? Are you really going to gather magic from other countries?'

'We're going to try to, yes,' Thordric said, levitating their luggage up onto the deck. 'According to Lyanis here, that's the only way we can free Vey safely.'

'Lyanis?' Batsu asked, looking down at her. She smiled at

54

him girlishly and, like Hamlet and Thordric, his face turned very pink. 'I don't believe we've met before, young lady,' he said, offering her a hand onto the ladder.

'Well, I would be amazed if we had, sir,' she said, still smiling at him. 'I've not been out of this forest for quite some time.' She batted her eyelashes at him, but Ourellus, who had climbed up behind her, shook her roughly.

'You have no idea how embarrassing it is to see you flirt with everyone, do you, mother? I know you look young, but maybe you should try acting your age for once,' he said huffily.

She smirked and flicked her long hair before sauntering off into the cabin. Wizard Batsu watched her incredulously. 'What did he mean by that?' he asked Thordric as Ourellus strolled off to help Kal lift Hamlet up, as he'd had some difficulty using the ladder.

'I'm not sure you want to know the full details, but I will say that she really is his mother and,' Thordric said, hesitating slightly, 'she's also my grandmother.'

'Your...grandmother? But then, if he's her son, doesn't that make him—'

Thordric lowered his eyes and made a small motion with his head.

'Oh,' was all Batsu managed to say.

Behind them came a loud crash as Hamlet fell onto the deck. Kal snorted and picked him up, ignoring his wincing. 'You know, Hamlet, perhaps you should get some more exercise. I don't think that doing field work alone will help you build enough muscle to climb properly,' he said.

Hamlet sniffed airily. 'I'll have you know that I take plenty of exercise. My hands were weak at the shock of everything that's happened, that's all.'

Everyone fought hard not to burst out laughing. Hamlet

was already fragile enough; openly mocking him would only do more damage. 'Oh, leave him alone, Kal,' Thordric said, helping Hamlet into the cabin. 'He wasn't the only one who struggled up the ladder. I was watching.'

Kal suddenly decided that the carvings on the ship's woodwork were far more interesting than discussing personal fitness.

Thordric turned back to Batsu. 'Shall we head off then? I need to tell the rest of the council what's going on and get some maps from the library.'

Batsu nodded and took to the ship's wheel, steering them away from Teroosa Forest and high up into the clouds, heading back to Jard Town. It'd been a difficult decision to leave Vey there alone, but Lyanis had assured them that he was perfectly safe in his frozen state, and it was very rare for any people to notice the forest. As Ourellus had hinted before, the magic that Lyanis had managed to store in the forest had only let Hamlet and Vey in because they posed no threat. Anyone wanting to harm the forest would either ignore it or find it too overbearing to stay there.

As the ship picked up speed, Lyanis came out of the cabin looking rather worried. 'Thordric, Hamlet asked me if you had any potion he could take. He really looked quite ill,' she said.

Thordric jumped violently. He had been deep in thought, wondering what the best way to get across the border would be. 'Here,' he said, handing her a vial of the anti-sickness potion. He had completely forgotten that Hamlet suffered as badly on ships as he did in carriages. Though he had to admit, at this speed, he couldn't blame him. Lyanis thanked him and went back to the cabin, where he could hear Hamlet moaning inside.

A few hours later, they arrived back in Jard Town, landing the ship in the courtyard of the council's turquoise, crescent-moon-shaped building. They disembarked quickly and made their way into the halls, which Lyanis took in with great interest.

Vey had recently replaced most of the paintings that had hung on the walls when Kalljard was around, but there were a few that he'd missed. One in particular, which was tucked around a corner near one of the store cupboards, was a full self-portrait.

Lyanis spotted it immediately, straying behind the rest of the group as they marched towards the meeting room. Thordric, sensing her missing, turned back to get her, with Ourellus in tow.

'Lyanis? Are you alright?' Thordric asked as they reached her. Then he saw the painting that held her focus.

'This is Kalljard, isn't it?' she said, staring at the tall, dark bearded man in the painting. Her eyes were wet, but the rest of her face was calm.

'Yes, it is,' he said. 'He looked like that right up until he died, apparently. Dark hair and all. But as soon as it, uh, *happened*...he went completely grey.' As he examined the painting himself, he saw that she and Kalljard had shared the same nose and mouth.

'Well, I can't say that I miss him,' Ourellus said loudly. 'I know he was my brother, but after everything he's done...I don't feel anything towards him except anger.'

Neither he nor Lyanis said anymore, so they hurried on to catch up with Hamlet and Kal. When they got to the meeting room, Lizzie was there waiting for them, along with the entire Wizard Council. Her greying hair, as usual when she was serious, had been swept up into a tight bun and she was wearing a long velvet dress, embroidered with the Wizard Council's symbol. She called for quiet, standing back to let Thordric address everyone, but as his eyes met hers, she looked at him with a mix of sympathy and pride. He knew then that either

Kal or Hamlet had told her about his connection to Ourellus and Lyanis.

He coughed as he stood up in front of the council. It seemed so long ago that he'd spoken to them about leaving to free Vey, even though it had only been the day before. 'Wizards of the council,' he began again. 'I'm afraid that freeing High Wizard Vey was not as easy a task as I was hoping. But there is a way, though I do not know how long it will take. Lyanis, who is Kalljard's mother—'

There were lots of gasps at this, as Lyanis stepped forwards so that they could see her properly. She was smiling broadly, until Ourellus dragged her to the back again, noticing how many of the wizards were mooning over her.

'I know she looks young, but she has revealed to us that she is a forest dweller and does not age as humans do. She was also frozen by Kalljard, before he founded Jard Town, and knows his magic well. The reason why High Wizard Vey became frozen in time is because he attempted to free her, and though he was successful in removing most of the spell, he was caught by Kalljard's trap spell.

'In order to break this trap spell without it being transferred onto anyone else, Lyanis has informed us that we must gather magic from four other countries, as she herself did to save Kalljard as an infant. Kalljard was imbued by these magics, which I can now reveal to you is the reason he was so strong.

'I know this must be hard to take in; after all, Kalljard didn't disclose anything about himself to anyone. Well, except maybe Rarn, and even then, it was probably what colour he preferred his toothbrush,' he joked, trying to the lighten the heavy mood that had swept over the room and remembering that Rarn had served mostly as Kalljard's chambermaid. A few wizards smiled weakly, but they were still in too much shock to react more than that.

'So, what the boy is trying to say,' said Lizzie, taking lead, 'Is that while he and his company are away, I will be remaining temporary head of the council.' From the way she spoke, Thordric had the distinct impression that she was enjoying herself. 'Please help them prepare for their travels in any way that you can,' she added as she motioned for everyone to leave.

'Thank you, Lizzie,' Thordric said, grinning at her. 'Er, I suppose I should introduce Lyanis to you properly...and now you know who Ourellus really is...'

'Don't worry,' she said. 'I won't tell your mother until all of this is cleared up. As far as she knows, you simply happened to find another wizard who wanted to help you with my poor Eric.'

She turned to Lyanis, who had been listening to her with interest. 'My husband told me a little about forest dwellers before he died. It seems that you're the only one left in this country. All the rest were chased out by Kalljard, or so he suspected, at least.'

Lyanis exhaled. 'It is as I feared then. Yet, I suppose in this age it matters not. Too much damage has been done to this land to pretend that it is worth them coming back.' She scrutinised Lizzie closely. So, you are High Wizard Vey's mother, are you? And you have no magic of your own?'

'Yes, I'm his mother, and it is correct that neither I, nor any women of this time possess any magic. Though,' she added, 'I sometimes wish I did, for it would certainly come in handy now and then.' She eyed the wizards still lingering in the room, one of whom was Wizard Ayek and a few of his friends. They were making no effort to conceal their dark glances at the two of them.

Lyanis sniffed and walked up to them, smiling sweetly. She whispered something to them and then laughed softly as each of them flushed a deep crimson and hurried from room.

'What did you say to them?' Lizzie asked curiously.

'Nothing that should be said in the presence of ladies such as yourself,' she said, her eyes twinkling naughtily. Ourellus heard her and groaned, sounding so much like Thordric that Lizzie laughed. Thordric knew what had amused her and scowled, scuttling out of the door, and leaving Hamlet and Kal to hurry after him.

In the library, the three of them searched for maps of the four neighbouring countries. Thordric was surprised to find that, though it had been thought that no one had travelled out of Dinia in centuries, there were books filled with details on all four. Uoo, it seemed, was full of nothing but forests, and apparently there were only a handful of humans living there. The rest were various species like the Watchem Watchems; small, twig-like creatures that disguised themselves as bushes; forest dwellers like Lyanis, and Criads, which resembled deer except for their human-like faces.

That was the country Lyanis suggested visiting first, as she was sure the Criads, whose magic it was that they needed, would willingly give it to them if they explained what they needed it for.

With interest, Thordric read on to find out more about the other countries. Fyoras was disgustingly hot, and they would have to travel across the vast expanse of desert by Neathin Valley to get there. Numteqa, which they could only get to by going over the mountains to the west, was very cold and full of carnivorous animals, and, to Thordric's mind more worrying, carnivorous plants too. The book he was reading described it as a place where you 'would either eat or be eaten', though the people who managed to survive there apparently brewed the best spirits in the world. Unfortunately, alcohol was banned in Dinia, due to the fact that it reacted badly with most forms of magic, and as nearly every household carried a stock of potions and spells made by the council, it would be incredibly dangerous for people to be allowed both.

The remaining country that they had to visit was Wyotis. It sounded quite similar to Dinia, though there were no towns and the people travelled across the land in giant wagons pulled by horses specially bred for their speed and strength. The only problem was that the people were split into five different tribes, each led by a young child born with purple eyes. There wasn't much detail on why this was, but from what he could gather, Thordric guessed it was these children who possessed the magic he would need. The five tribes were almost continually at war with each other, so the children were protected by great measures to ensure that they weren't captured by the enemy.

'Looks like we're in for an interesting journey,' Kal said dryly over Thordric's shoulder, scanning the page that he'd been reading. 'Still, I'll be able to practice my magic along the way.'

'Actually, Kal,' Thordric said uneasily. 'I'm thinking it would be best of you didn't come with us.'

'What? Why?' he exclaimed, searching Thordric's face for an answer.

Thordric couldn't bring himself to tell him that he was worried Kal's hunger for magic would take over like Lyanis had warned. 'It's going to be dangerous. I'm not sure you're prepared for that.'

'You didn't think that when you asked me to help you sort out that rockslide four months ago. We were right on the cliff, and if it'd crumbled neither of us would have survived,' Kal accused.

Thordric's cheeks went pink. He had indeed put Kal in

danger back then, having been in such a rush to help that he hadn't thought twice about his friend's safety.

'You've got to let me help you, Thordric. I can; you know I can. I might not have as much control over my magic as the rest of the council, but I can do it if I try properly.'

'I...I'll think about it,' Thordric said, though he knew he couldn't refuse him any longer.

8

THE JOURNEY BEGINS

L oading up *Dinia's Jewel* took far longer than they expected, as not only did they have to take all the maps and books concerning each country, but several large cases of potions in case they got injured or became ill.

Lizzie had also made sure that they had packed plenty of warm clothing for when they went to Numteqa, especially for Lyanis, who preferred to walk around in the lightest possible attire she could find. It had taken a long-winded argument with Lizzie to convince her that she'd freeze if she didn't wear thicker clothing in Numteqa, but eventually Lizzie won through and filled two large cases for her.

They packed plenty of food too, with most of it under a stasis spell to make sure it wouldn't rot. When Thordric had cast the spell, it struck him how similar it was to the frozen in time spell of Kalljard's, though the simple stasis spell could only freeze things that were no longer living.

By the time everything was in, everyone was famished, so they had one last meal at the council before they left. It was considerably better prepared than normal, because Lizzie'd had quite a large hand in preparing it and, as usual when she cooked, not only was it all delicious but there was plenty of it; so much in fact that nearly the whole Council were able to have second helpings, and pudding too if they wanted it.

Stuffed and ready to begin their journey, and after saying goodbye to everyone, Hamlet, Ourellus, Lyanis, Kal and Thordric headed to the ship, preparing to embark.

But before Thordric could climb up on deck, Kal took him to one side, making sure that the others were safely out of earshot. Thordric looked at him; he was rather pale and clammy, and had been oddly quiet at dinner, even after Thordric had consented to let him go with them. His dreadlocks even seemed to be hanging more limply than normal.

'Thordric, there's...something that I've been meaning to tell you. I didn't want to because I knew you'd be angry, but I can't stand hiding it any longer,' Kal said, shaking as though what he was about to say was the most difficult thing he'd ever had to do.

'Go on,' Thordric said. 'Whatever it is, I'll listen.'

Kal took a deep breath. 'Hamlet didn't find Teroosa Forest by himself...well, not entirely. You see, when I used the long-distance communicator to ask him to bring me the plant I needed for my potion, I asked him where he was. He told me that he was on his way back, but he couldn't see any of the plant I needed in sight. I knew Teroosa Forest was nearby, I'd read about it in another one of Kalljard's journals hidden in the room at the end of the passage you found. It mentioned the forest's location, and the fact that he had sealed something there. I knew that if Hamlet saw it, he would probably tell High Wizard Vey and I hoped that it would be interesting enough for him to want to see it himself.'

'But why?' Thordric asked, confused. 'Do you mean that you wanted to get Vey away from the council?'

Kal lowered his gaze, staring at his feet. 'I knew about his plans to name you as the next High Wizard in his *Wishes Upon Death or Retirement;* I overheard him talking to Inspector Jimmson about it when he made his annual visit a few weeks ago.' He shifted uncomfortably. 'I was jealous of you. I know Kalljard was a monster, but he was my father and the previous High Wizard. I felt like I had more right to be the future High Wizard than you, and so I wanted Vey out of the way so that I could try and convince the rest of the council that he was making a mistake by naming you.'

Thordric was speechless, but then he laughed and hit Kal around the head with one of the extra maps he had hastily grabbed at the last minute to take with them. 'You blockhead! What a ridiculous thing to get jealous about! Even if Vey has named me as the next High Wizard, he won't be stepping down for at least twenty years yet. Anything could happen in that time. Perhaps you will be better suited to it than me when you grow up a bit more and have a better grasp of your magic.'

'You're not angry?' Kal said in disbelief.

'No, just surprised,' Thordric said, hoping Kal wouldn't see through his lie. The young wizard's confession had disappointed him deeply, but what was done was done.

'But it's my fault that High Wizard Vey is now like he is,' Kal said. Thordric's reaction was so different from what he'd been expecting that he was sure Thordric had misunderstood.

'No, it's not,' Thordric said seriously, putting a hand on his shoulder. He had meant it to be a consoling gesture, but the sleeves of his robes were so long that he had to fumble with them to pull them up enough to do it. Kal managed a smile. 'You might have been the one who ultimately led Vey to the forest, but you couldn't have known what he would try to do,' he continued, letting go and watching his sleeve droop down again almost immediately.

'I suppose not,' Kal mumbled.

'Then there's no need to dwell on it,' Thordric said.

Kal seemed to cheer up after that and scurried off up the ladder onto the deck to catch the bundle of maps that Thordric levitated up after him.

The journey east to Uoo wasn't very long. It joined up with the border at Dinia's narrowest point, barely two days away with the speed of *Dinia's Jewel*. The moment they crossed the border, marked with heavy pillars made of onyx and spread at mile long intervals, the air became dense with insects and species of bird that only Lyanis and Ourellus had ever seen.

'They used to migrate to Dinia in the winter. They regularly came to my forest, and all the other forests that used to be there. I don't know what Kalljard did, but there's obviously some reason why they don't cross the border anymore,' Lyanis explained. She glanced back at one of the pillars they had passed. 'They weren't here the last time I came to Uoo, I'm sure of it.'

Thordric gazed at the pillar – now barely a dot in the distance – too. He had felt something as they'd gone past it, but the feeling had been so subtle that he'd barely even registered it. Perhaps he would investigate the pillars when they had more time.

Giant trees grew up around them now, and Ourellus, who was steering as though he'd been doing it his whole life, had to swerve around their wide trunks to prevent *Dinia's Jewel* from crashing into them. As well as trees, there were also thick vines that they had to avoid, linking almost every tree. Small furry creatures scurried along them, their fur coloured various shades of purple.

All the greenery was so dense that it was difficult to see

anything else, even when they looked overboard, because the ground was hidden from view by the tops of smaller trees.

'How far in do we need to go, mother?' Ourellus asked, turning to Lyanis.

'Ask your son,' she replied. 'He's got all the maps.'

Ourellus looked over at Thordric, trying to hide the flush creeping up his face. Thordric felt his own face grow hot, and hastily opened up the large map of Uoo he had and hid behind it. He still couldn't believe that a man who looked barely older than him was his father, no matter how much they resembled each other.

Finally, after a long silence that stretched several minutes while he studied the map, he reappeared. 'According to this, the Criads live in only one part of the country. Fortunately for us, it's about another day's travel at most.'

Everyone sighed, except for Hamlet, who was locked away in the cabin with several bottles of anti-sickness potion.

A few more hours passed, with everyone busying themselves with different things. Thordric was jumping between studying the maps and going through his notes on his dishwashing spell. Lyanis and Ourellus were talking among themselves as he continued to steer the ship, and Kal had decided it was best to get a few hours' sleep.

After a while, Ourellus let Lyanis take over the wheel, which she found delightful, despite narrowly missing a low hanging branch. After he had made sure she knew what she was doing, he came to sit by Thordric. Thordric ignored him.

Ourellus coughed slightly. In a way that made it appear a great effort, Thordric finally looked up at him. 'What is it?' he said, somewhat harshly.

'I...thought we should talk,' Ourellus said awkwardly.

Thordric glared, but then gave in. 'Fine, what do you want to talk about?'

'Well, I, er...' Ourellus began, trying to ignore the way Thordric's eyebrow had shot up. 'How is your mother?' he managed eventually.

'She's fine. She lives not far from the stationhouse, actually, with the inspector and my little sisters.'

Ourellus looked crestfallen. 'You mean she remarried?'

'Yes, and happily so, so you keep your nose out of it,' he snapped. He knew he was being childish, but suddenly meeting his father for the first time in his life with the most complicated explanation as to why was more than a little over-whelming.

'I'm glad she's happy,' Ourellus said quietly. 'I really did love her, you know. Had I have known what would happen, and that she would be having you...perhaps I would have been more careful.'

He sniffed, and Thordric saw that there were large tears in his eyes. He rummaged around in his pockets and handed Ourellus a faded handkerchief.

'It...was a long time ago,' Thordric said, watching Ourellus wipe the tears away. 'But she never knew what happened to you, and over the years she fell silent about it. The only thing she told me was that you were a wizard.'

He looked at Ourellus, trying to think of a way to change the subject. 'Back when you told us what happened to you, you said that Kalljard began hating other half-wizards. What I can't understand is, *why* did he? I thought no one took any notice of things like that back then,' Thordric asked.

'I'm not sure either,' Ourellus replied. 'There was no real training for anyone like you have at the council today. Everyone had to find out how to master their magic on their own, and there were many mistakes and accidents with both full and half-wizards. Perhaps he just wanted a way to get into power, and by making the people fear them he found he could control people with that fear.'

'Well, there is that,' Lyanis said over their shoulder, making them both jump and panic about who was steering. They saw that Kal had taken the wheel and was doing a good job of guiding the ship in the oncoming darkness. 'I do seem to remember a group of half-wizards who took pity on him because he had been ill, though. If there's anything he despised more, it was having people feel sorry for him,' she continued, sitting down next to them, and rummaging through one of the bags of food, pulling out a lumpy, brown fruit known for its delicate sweetness.

She bit into it, wiping away the juice that ran down her chin with relish. 'So, have you two taken to each other a little better?' she asked.

They glanced at each other sheepishly and mumbled a 'yes'.

'Good,' she said. 'For a while I thought that your animosity would last for the whole journey, which would have made it even worse.'

The ship was far too cramped for her liking, and though she was happy that they were among the trees, the fact that her feet had not yet touched the soil irked her.

With Ourellus steering once more and conferring with Thordric about their location every few minutes, they reached the location where the Criads were thought to be early the next morning.

They lowered the ship as much as they could, its hull skimming across several brightly coloured bushes that gurgled as they passed. Thordric had a hunch that they were really

Watchem Watchems, for no real bushes gurgled like that when they were rustled.

They came to a stop by a small lake, which looked as though it could be the main source of water for many of the forest's creatures to come and drink from. Lyanis jumped to the ground before they could even get the ladder down, wriggling her toes in the earth. Thordric saw several mouse-like creatures running towards her, but on closer inspection they appeared to be living balls of cotton wool. They climbed up her legs and onto her shoulders, and she cooed at them gently.

'What are they?' he asked, climbing down the ladder to stand beside her.

'They're Olymps,' she said. 'When a forest like this one is healthy and full of life, they always gather there. If you look closely, you'll see that there are hundreds watching us right now.'

He looked around him closely and saw that she was right. Under almost every leaf and bit of exposed root were white tufts of cotton wall, looking at them with large black eyes.

Lyanis held one up to her ear, making several popping sounds with her mouth. Thordric heard the Olymp make the same sounds back, though it was so quiet he had to strain his ears.

'You can talk to them?' he said, after she had done it several times more.

'Of course I can. All forest dwellers can understand the animals here,' she said, as though it were obvious.

'What did it say, then?'

'*He* says that the Criads will be here around midday. That's when they usually come to drink,' she replied.

9

CRIADS AND FOREST DWELLERS

They waited by the lake for midday to come around, with Lyanis entertaining them by pointing out all the animals that went there to drink.

There were foxes with tails of feathers, something that resembled a large tree trunk that slithered on the ground, two headed snakes, and a creature Thordric thought was a giant insect, but turned out to be a small mole-like animal with a disguise of various twigs and leaves on its back. They drank one after another, waiting patiently for the other to finish as though there were some unspoken law that only one species may go at a time.

As the morning passed and, by Hamlet's mechanical watch (enhanced by Thordric some years ago so that it only needed to be wound every six months), it neared midday, they heard a loud rustling in the trees behind them. They all grew hopeful, hoping that the Criads had come at last, but instead three people edged out of the bushes.

The light hit their skin, and Thordric saw that it was the same silvery grey as Lyanis's. Were they also forest dwellers?

He watched Lyanis's eyes narrow as she scrutinized them. Two were male; one was so tall that they all had to tilt their heads back to see his face. He had deep lines around his mouth and brow that emphasized his stern expression. The other looked like a stockier version of Kal, complete with dreadlocks, though his were down to his thighs and tied back with a length of vine.

The third was female, as youthful seeming as Lyanis herself, except there was a soft, greenish glow coming from her. Thordric wondered if it was because she *was* young, rather than merely appearing that way.

'I never thought to see *you* here again, Lyanis,' the tall male said, his voice crackling like dry leaves. 'Tell me, was it true that you were frozen by that son of yours?'

'Yes,' Lyanis replied, with a steely hint to her voice. 'I was trapped for a thousand years but freed recently by this boy.' She gestured to Thordric, who stepped forwards politely to say hello, but retreated quickly at the withering stare all three of them gave him.

'We told you not to fool around with those humans,' the one with dreadlocks said, accusingly.

'I did not "fool around" with them, I fell in love and had sons. There is no crime in that,' she said.

'Of course there is,' the dreadlocked one spat. 'Your duty is to your forest, not to your heart. And if it was love you were looking for, then why did you not seek someone of your own kind; I gave you plenty of opportunities—'

'Enough, Kyik,' the tall one said, and Kyik fell silent, looking abashed. 'What is it you seek from here now, Lyanis?' he asked, his voice still hard. 'Do not tell me that you seek the Criads' sacred antlers again, after you so foolishly wasted them before on that sickly child of yours?'

'She didn't waste them!' Ourellus snapped, stepping forwards defiantly. 'They helped to save my brother's life.'

'And look what he became, imbued with such power. Do not try to tell me that saving a monster like that is justified, boy,' the tall one snapped back. 'I was there when he took over. The place where he founded his town used to be my home. But he burnt it all with his magic and chased every living creature out, including those tribes that were of his own kind.

'I, along with Kyik and many others, retreated to this country to die peacefully under the gentle eyes of our native cousins here, but instead they chose to accept us and allowed us to help care for this forest as we did for our own,' he said, his grey eyes burning.

The young woman next to him gently put her hand on his arm and, for few seconds, the greenish light around her intensified. The fire in his eyes subdued, and the lines on his face became more relaxed. 'You're right, Emaya,' he said softly. 'I should not let my temper rise in these parts, for the Criads would not like it.'

He turned back to Lyanis and Ourellus, surveying them. 'The Criads may take pity on you once again, Lyanis, but if you abuse their generosity, then we shall never forgive you.'

They said no more and turned on their heels, disappearing back among the foliage. Lyanis sank to her knees. Giant, fat tears rolled down her face. She began muttering something in a different language, gripping the ground with her hands.

'What is she doing?' Hamlet whispered to Thordric and Kal. They both shrugged, but Ourellus sprang forwards and pulled her up.

'No, mother! You can't do that!' he said, shaking her violently. 'We still need your help.'

'What is it?' Thordric said, coming forwards.

'She was asking the forest to take the life from her...she was trying to kill herself.'

The others gasped and ran towards her side. She looked at them, shaking. 'It was true. It was all true. I should have remained in my forest, protecting it from harm and ignored the people who became lost. I have disgraced our kind.'

As she spoke, six large creatures came out of the trees. Thordric had to blink twice. Of all the creatures he had seen that day, these were the most magnificent, yet bizarre, of them all.

They were at least the size of a house, shaped very much like deer, but instead of short tan-coloured fur, they were covered in long trailing moss that hid their hooves and, as Thordric studied their long necks, he saw that the moss gently receded to become small, tightly linked scales coloured a mottled blue. The scales covered their entire faces, which, though slightly more angular, looked very human. There were also long antlers protruding from the top of each one's head, curved and sharp, pulsing with a dull light.

They must be the Criads!

As Thordric, Hamlet, Kal and Ourellus stared, they realised that the Criads were also examining them. The one closest made a great rumbling sound with its mouth. It stopped and looked at them, then tried again, slightly different this time. When they didn't respond, a frown appeared on its large, scaly face.

One of the Criads further back went up to it and made a short rumbling into its ear. The first one looked back at it in surprise, and then, glancing down at them all still standing there watching this strange communication, it broke out into Dinian. Its voice was low and expressive, sounding male.

'So, you're humans, are you?' he said to them, obviously amused. 'You look a little different to what I expected, so you will forgive me for not realising immediately. I am known as Hin, leader of the Criads.' He stopped, spotting Lyanis, who was still lying on the ground crying soundlessly. 'Is that you, Lyanis?'

Lyanis looked up at him. 'Yes, Hin,' she managed, wiping away her tears. 'I have come back to ask you for the same favour as before, if you find us worthy enough.'

'You are sad,' Hin said, lowering his neck and nudging her gently with his face. 'Come back with us, and we shall listen.'

He spoke to the other Criads in the same rumbling language as before, and they all lowered their haunches to the ground so that Thordric's party could climb onto their backs. 'What about the ship?' Kal asked, nervously touching one of the Criad's mossy fur. It squelched in his hand, but somehow, he remained quite dry.

'It will be safe,' Hin told him. 'No creature here will touch it.'

Reassured, they all climbed onto the Criads' backs, their stomachs lurching slightly as the Criads stood up and flicked their legs to readjust themselves to the weight. Then the Criads began to move, and Thordric, Hamlet and Kal all had to grab hold of the moss to keep from falling off. Kal noticed that both Thordric and Hamlet had to reach inside their pockets for the anti-sickness potion, drinking it down quickly.

Lyanis and Ourellus were both riding the Criads as if it was the most comfortable thing in the world, swaying with the Criads' weight changes, hardly gripping on at all.

The Criads took them into a much denser part of the forest, where the trees, that so far had all been normal evergreens and pines, now became all sorts of colours, reminding Thordric of the trees in the garden of the Wizard Council. He wondered if Kalljard had gathered seeds from here and taken them back before he'd closed the borders, for they certainly didn't grow wild anywhere in Dinia.

Some of the trees had large, bulbous pods on them, which Hin advised them to avoid as they contained a liquid that was highly poisonous to humans. Kal, who had been about to reach out and grab one, snatched his hand back quickly and gulped.

After an hour had passed, and Thordric felt he was getting the hang of balancing properly on the Criad's back, they came to a large clearing surrounded by rainbow-coloured trees. The Criads knelt again, allowing them all to get off, and went to the edge of the trees. They blew on them gently, causing the branches to merge so that they were completely closed in.

Then Hin walked over to a small pile of rocks that were in the centre and blew on those too. Instantly, they glowed a deep red and let out as much heat as a fire, warming the cool forest air. Thordric and the others gladly gathered around them, realising that their skin felt like ice.

'Tell me, Lyanis,' Hin said as he and the other Criads sat down around them. 'Why is it that you and these humans seek our sacred antlers once more?'

Lyanis took a deep breath, and then explained what Kalljard had done to her and Ourellus, and how High Wizard Vey had tried to free them and become frozen in time himself. Hin listened intently, making no comment until she had finished.

'It seems that fate has indeed dealt you a foul hand,' he said afterwards. There was a murmur of agreement from the other Criads. 'Yet I do not believe that you made the wrong choice in saving Kalljard. If you had let him die, then you would have suffered for the rest of your life.'

He took a breath, shaking his mossy fur. 'I shall give you a pair of our sacred antlers gladly, for shedding them has no great consequence for us. But,' he said, his keen gaze darting between Ourellus, Kal and Thordric, 'we must give it to the right person this time, lest it cause the same hunger for power that Kalljard suffered from.' He put his head forwards, indicating Kal. Come forwards, young one,' he said.

Kal stood up nervously, but with that same glint in his eyes that Thordric had seen before. He walked over to Hin and spoke to him, but somehow their conversation was silent to the others. After a few minutes, Kal came back and sat down again wordlessly. Before he could say anything, Hin called Thordric up to him. Thordric went, a knot in his stomach, hoping that Hin would spare him from whatever it was that he'd told Kal, because it was obviously not pleasant.

'So, you are Lyanis's other grandson,' Hin said as Thordric reached him. 'You possess a good deal of power already, though it is different to that of young Kal's. I can sense that you do not feel it makes you superior to other humans. This is a trait which has served you well. I was thinking of giving the sacred antlers to your father but given that he has not used his magic for so many years, the power of the antlers might be too much for him. You, however, should be able to control it with ease. Yet I must warn you not to reveal it to the creatures in the other countries that you wish to travel to, for they will take it from you without hesitation and use it for their own means.'

Hin bent down his head so that his antlers were level with Thordric. 'Place your hand on my antlers, Thordric,' he said. 'If I am right, then you will be able to take their power within you and feel as though they are purely an extension of your own magic.'

Thordric swallowed and stretched out his hand. The antlers pulsed more brightly, then disappeared. A strong warmth flowed through Thordric's body, and he felt like he understood magic much more than he had before, as if any thought or idea he had could be made a reality. He realised how easily it would have been for this power to take over Kal, and though the thought made him sad, he was glad that Hin had decided Kal was not suited for it.

'Now you have what you seek,' Hin said to all of them. His antlers, they all realised, had grown back already, and were pulsing dully once more. 'Now we shall take you back so that you can continue your journey.'

He motioned for them to climb onto the Criads' backs once more, and as soon as they were mounted, he and the other Criads blew on the trees again, making them withdraw their branches so that the path out of the clearing opened back up.

Everyone was silent on the return journey to the lake, and even when they dismounted and said a grateful farewell to Hin and the other Criads, they only spoke enough to decide who would steer the ship first while the others rested.

Kal had retreated into the cabin with Hamlet, leaving only Thordric, Ourellus and Lyanis up on deck. They offered him some food a few hours later, but he flatly refused it, so they left him alone.

'What do you think Hin said to him?' Thordric said at last, picking at his own bread roll and watching Lyanis guide the ship around a wayward branch.

Ourellus looked at him. 'Only the truth, I expect. That Kal has inherited a great deal of his father's personality, which, as mother warned you before, could become a serious problem for him...and for us, if we allow it to. However, perhaps now that he knows it, he will try to control his urges himself without us interfering; for at the heart of it, Kal is the only one capable of preventing himself from giving in to the darkness within him.'

10

SHIELD PRACTICE

'Which way is the quickest to get to Fyoras?' Ourellus asked, now steering the ship himself while Lyanis slept. His question was directed at Thordric, who was pouring over the maps again, wrapped under several cloaks that had sheltered him from the downpour they'd just experienced. The rain had been so sudden that he hadn't time to put up a shield against it.

'Well, we could cut through from the north of Uoo, but by the looks of it, there's a volcano near there. In the books I've read, they say that it sends up ash clouds almost every month. I'm not sure it's a good idea to go through it, even if we do put a barrier up around *Dinia's Jewel*.'

'Is there another way that's safer?' Ourellus said, steering away from a giant branch littered with silver-coloured nuts. He reached out to pick some as they passed and threw one to Thordric. 'Don't worry,' he added. 'They're not poisonous; I've seen them growing in mother's forest before.'

Thordric bit into it thankfully, surprised at the sweet, caramel-like flavour that it had. He chewed it, looking back at his map. 'There is another way,' he said, swallowing. 'We can cross the border from Neathin Valley. There's a desert a few miles from the town, and according to this, it runs straight into Fyoras.'

'Neathin Valley is in north Dinia, isn't it?' Ourellus asked, leaning over to look at the map himself.

Thordric nodded. 'If we cross back over the border and keep going north, we'll reach it. We might even cross paths with *The Jardine*.'

'What's *The Jardine*?' Ourellus asked, intrigued.

'It's the biggest ship in the fleet of the floating Ships of Kal. I travelled to Neathin Valley on it three years ago – it's where I first met Hamlet. Kal's foster father is the captain of it.'

Ourellus smiled. 'I do find these ships interesting, there was nothing like this around before Kalljard took over. If you wanted to get on a ship, you had to travel to the border between Wyotis and Uoo, where there's about two miles that opens out to the sea. Most of it was used as a dockyard, back when we still traded with other countries.'

Thordric was surprised. He hadn't known that any part of Dinia connected to the ocean, but then again, he hadn't travelled anywhere apart from the places he had been sent to by the Wizard Council.

After discussing the situation with Lyanis and Hamlet, Thordric made the decision to cross the border into Dinia again and travel up to Neathin Valley. Kal still refused to talk to anyone, though he'd appeared interested when they mentioned going there.

His foster father and mother lived in Neathin Valley with their daughter Lily, who was a little sister to him, even if she had used to laugh at his magic. He hadn't seen her properly since he'd joined the council, only catching glimpses when she'd hitched a ride on *The Jardine* with her father, Captain Jal, which her mother resented purely because she didn't like Lily to see Kal at all. She was of the opinion that Kal was dangerous, an idea that Thordric had tried to rid her of many times.

As they sailed over the countryside, Thordric tried to think of a way to make Kal cheer up. He couldn't say that what Hin had told him didn't matter, because it did, but perhaps there was a way to make him think more positively about it.

He knocked on the cabin door, which was answered by Hamlet. Despite taking the anti-sickness potion every day, he still hadn't been able to face staying on deck.

'What is it, Thordric?' he said weakly.

'Can you ask Kal to come out?' Thordric asked, looking into the room. Kal had his back to the door and was pretending to be deeply absorbed in a book about the geography of Fyoras.

'I can try,' Hamlet replied, his voice lacking confidence. He closed the door and went back into the room. Thordric heard him speak to Kal, but there was no reply. Hamlet opened the door again and spread his arms: no luck.

'What if I told him that I would like to teach him some magic?' Thordric said, loud enough for Kal to hear. He turned around and looked at Thordric, trying to determine whether he was telling the truth or not. Thordric grinned back at him.

'Fine,' Kal said, snapping the book shut. He walked past Hamlet out onto the deck. 'What spell is it that you want me to learn?'

'I don't know. I thought I'd let you choose,' Thordric replied. The corners of Kal's mouth twitched slightly.

'I don't know how to make a shield yet,' he said, trying not to sound too interested.

'Then I'll teach you that,' Thordric replied, less confidently than he felt. Shielding was something that he had only learnt himself the year before, and it had proved very difficult to master, even with Vey coaching him. He looked over at Lyanis, who had sat up among her bed of makeshift covers to watch them. 'Would you like to help?' he asked her.

'If I can,' she smiled. 'What would you like me to do?'

'I need you to throw things at us,' Thordric said, making her laugh. 'Only when I tell you to, though; I need to go over the theory first.'

He scratched the short beard that was sprouting from his chin, thinking how best to explain it. 'Objects fall because of gravity,' he began. Kal rolled his eyes at him; he'd known that much when he was little. 'A shield works as a way of pushing back at that force, so that whatever object is falling at you, even if it's rain or hail, it acts like an umbrella, making the object fall to the side. A strong shield can cover a large area from all angles, though I'm afraid I'm not practiced enough to do that yet myself.

'So, the first thing I want you to think about is pushing upwards with your magic. I'll hold my hand above your head, and if you can move it up, then you'll have the basics.'

For the next two hours, Kal practiced doing just that, though it took him nearly the whole time to move Thordric's hand a fraction away. Thordric encouraged him, saying that he'd struggled as much when he was learning it. In fact, Kal was actually doing slightly better, for Thordric's first time trying had sent Vey flying up into the ceiling, and it had taken three days to figure out how to stop using so much force; for while a shield had to be strong, the strength needed to be spread out over a wide area. Thordric's trouble had been that he was trying to pinpoint the force too much.

They broke for lunch, discussing how to refine it so that Kal didn't use too little or too much force, and Ourellus surprised them by saying that he'd never even thought of learning how to make a shield.

'No one really used them back then. If it rained or snowed,

or if something was about to fall on your head or be thrown at you, people simply dodged it,' he told them. 'Though I admit, there was one time when I was sitting under a tree reading that a large fruit fell down and hit me on the head. I was unconscious for half a day because of it.'

'Well, it probably would have hit me too,' Thordric admitted. 'It takes me almost a minute to get my shields stable enough to work. I am good at levitating though, so if it's a single object, I can usually focus on it and levitate it away from me.' He remembered the time when he'd had to do it while he had been staying in Neathin Valley. An untrained half-wizard named Grale had attacked the house where he'd been staying by using magic to throw large tree branches, and needing to act quickly, Thordric had caught them with his own magic and levitated them away.

'Why don't you practice along with Kal, then, if your shields are so bad?' Lyanis suggested. 'I'm sure I can manage to throw things at the both of you.'

Thordric raised his eyebrow at her but agreed that it was a good idea. They stood up and prepared their shields while she gathered several large books and a pair of extra boots from their luggage bags.

'Are you ready?' she called, grinning unashamedly. Thordric and Kal gritted their teeth. She threw the first book at Thordric's head. It bounced off his shield and onto Kal's one, but it fell through, barely missing his toes.

He groaned but had to focus again immediately as Lyanis threw the next one. Again, it bounced off Thordric's shield and onto his. This time it held for a few seconds, but sustaining it was difficult and it dropped through to the ground a moment later.

'Do you want to rest?' Thordric asked him, knowing how much effort it took at first.

Kal grimaced at him. 'Only if you do,' he said, and tried raising his shield again. Thordric saw the determination in his eyes and smiled. A few weeks ago, Kal would have complained that it was too much strain and pushed off practice until the next day but listening to Hin had obviously affected him in more ways than one.

The day went on, and both of them kept it up until night-fall. However, when Thordric decided that Kal had definitely done enough for one day and sent him back into the cabin to rest, he asked for Lyanis to help him practice by himself.

He had felt the magic of the Criads' sacred antlers trying to break free all day, but he hadn't wanted to use it in front of Kal in case it upset him again. Now, however, he couldn't wait to try it.

Lyanis readied the boot she was holding, telling him to prepare, but instead of waiting until he was ready, he asked her to throw it at will. She obliged, and as the boot sailed towards his head, he put up his shield, drawing upon the magic of the scared antlers. It stabilised immediately and the boot bounced straight off. It had been completely effortless; he hadn't even needed to use his will at all. It was like it worked at the merest thought, something that was impossible with wizard magic. Even Vey, who looked as though he used his magic fluently, had to put serious effort in to use it properly.

'Try it again, Lyanis,' he said, wondering how quickly he could do it. This time, the boot had hardly left her hand before his shield was up. He gulped. This really *was* powerful magic.

'Perhaps I should try throwing several things at once,' Lyanis said, disappointed that he had blocked it so quickly. He agreed and she threw three books at him, all of which sailed in different directions, testing the evenness of his shield. Yet all three bounced off and fell to the floor.

Excited, he suddenly fell straight down towards the floor,

putting up a shield just before he hit it. It held him there, barely an inch away from the wooden boards. 'This is amazing!' he said, and began trying dangerous stunts one after the other, managing to shield himself from injury every time. Then he stopped and coughed, embarrassed by his sudden display as Lyanis and Ourellus laughed at him.

Four days passed by the time they arrived in Neathin Valley, and as they came closer to the docks where *The Jardine* usually anchored, they saw that it was about to leave.

Ourellus and Lyanis marvelled at it; decorated a deep purple with sails coloured silver, it was the most magnificent thing they had ever seen. Hamlet even managed to come out on deck to have a look, gazing wide eyed like the first time he'd seen it. Despite feeling ill every time he stepped onboard one, Hamlet had a special fondness for ships. In fact, as Kalljard had left it unnamed, Vey had let Hamlet name *Dinia's Jewel* when they'd found it in the cargo hold of *The Jardine* because he loved them so much.

At Thordric's request, Ourellus steered *Dinia's Jewel* next to *The Jardine*, so that they were parallel with the deck. Captain Jal, spying them from his cabin, came out to see them. 'Wizard Thordric,' he said, mistaking Ourellus for him. 'What are you doing in these parts?'

Thordric came forwards so that Captain Jal did a double take. 'This is my, er, friend, Ourellus,' Thordric explained, introducing him. 'He's a relative of mine.'

'Oh, then please accept my pardon, sir,' Jal said to Ourellus. 'I simply thought that Wizard Thordric had grown a lot since I last saw him.'

Feeling uncomfortable, Thordric hastily changed the

subject. 'Unfortunately, we're not staying in Neathin Valley, we've got business in Fyoras, so we've come to cross border.'

'You're travelling out of the country?' Jal asked, intrigued.

'Yes,' Thordric began, but before he could say anymore, Kal came out of the cabin. He spotted Captain Jal and promptly jumped off *Dinia's Jewel* and onto the deck of *The Jardine* to embrace him.

'Kal? I thought you were supposed to be training back at the council?' Jal said, surprised at Kal's sudden show of affection. 'Is everything alright?'

Kal broke away from him, downcast, but Thordric took over for him. 'We've been working on some new magic, and it's made for tricky learning,' he said, not entirely telling the truth. The shielding spell was difficult, and it was true that Kal was still struggling with it, but Thordric knew that it was Hin's words that were playing on Kal's mind. Seeing his foster father again had obviously come as a great comfort to him.

'Oh, I see,' Jal said, not really understanding due to his lack of magical knowledge. 'So, you're frustrated, then?' he asked Kal.

'A bit,' Kal replied, glancing gratefully up at Thordric. 'Is Lily onboard at all?' he asked, looking around.

Jal shook his head. 'No, she's started working with your mother at the springs. Though I don't think she's too keen on it; she says the customers always complain that the water's too hot, despite knowing it's a hot spring. You could stop in on them if you have time,' he said.

'I'm afraid we can't,' Thordric said. 'We have to get going soon. Perhaps we'll come back after our business is finished.'

He motioned for Kal to get back on board, and with a wave they said farewell and steered *Dinia's Jewel* onwards over the town of Valley Edge; situated on the edge of Neathin Valley itself; whose brightly coloured houses looked like some bizarre patchwork quilt covering the land.

Lyanis cast her eye overboard at it. 'I seem to remember this all being a forest at one time,' she said, frowning. She glanced over to the valley itself, which was cracked and dry like a groove in a particularly old bit of tree bark. 'There used to be a great river running through there, too, though it looks as if it's been dry for many years.'

'It has,' Hamlet said next to her. 'The ancient tribe known as the Neathers destroyed all the forest to get rid of their enemies, who depended upon it for survival. Without the trees to shelter the land from the sun, it gradually dried out. Thordric and Vey managed to restore a small part of it after Kal accidentally set off some dormant magic here, but without the river, it'd be hard to return it to how it once was.'

'How do you know this place anyway, mother?' Ourellus asked shrewdly.

'We forest dwellers used to get together every now and then, and I was invited here at one time,' she replied.

Ourellus narrowed his eyes at her, but she smiled at him impishly and looked away.

11

SWEAT AND PROMISES

They passed through Neathin Valley without stopping, though everyone except Lyanis wanted to get off the ship so they could find somewhere to wash. None of them, especially Thordric and Kal, were used to going this long without a bath. Lyanis laughed at them, saying that the only time for washing was when it rained.

As she wasn't human, she didn't sweat like they did, and simply couldn't understand what was making them feel so grimy. She did, however, notice the distinct whiff of week-old body odour radiating from them, but far from being repulsed, she thought it was pleasant.

'It's your natural smell. I don't see why you should be ashamed of that,' she told Thordric, Kal and Hamlet after they'd had a particularly long discussion about what they would all do at the first sight of water. Unfortunately, they were now flying over a vast desert which carried on far across the border into Fyoras, so it would be at least another three days before they found even the merest trickle. 'And you,' she said to Ourellus, who was also feeling distinctly dirty and itchy, 'shouldn't be complaining either. I don't remember you ever washing except during a downpour when you were a child.'

'That was then, before I knew how good being clean felt,' he said defensively, as Thordric shot him a disgusted look.

Lyanis pouted and sat down next to the food bag, rummaging around for more of the bobbled fruit. The sun was scorching hot now, heating the planks of the ship so that it burnt their hands if they touched the wood for too long. Their water flasks were also nearly empty; they'd had to ration it out, so they had enough to last until they got to Fyoras.

No one was happy about the situation, and their conversation had become snappy and waspish. Hamlet stayed in the cabin reading, and Ourellus and Lyanis spoke about times before they'd been frozen. Kal and Thordric had given up practicing their shielding spell, as neither of them had the energy to do it. Instead, they played a game of chess, betting that the loser would be the one to wring the sweat out of the other's clothing. Kal was good at chess, seeing opportunities and taking them before Thordric could even remember how each piece could be used.

So far, Thordric had wrung out Kal's clothes five times already. It was foul, but at least it gave them something to do while they waited to reach the border.

At the end of the third day, after Thordric had had to do this gruesome task once more, they saw the giant black pillars carved from onyx that marked the border between Dinia and Fyoras.

As they passed through, Thordric felt the subtle magic coming from them again. Being closer to one of them now, he reached out and laid his hand upon it, but recoiled instantly with a yelp.

'What's the matter?' Ourellus said sharply, taking Thordric's arm and examining it from elbow to fingertips. There was no wound, not even a scratch.

'I heard it,' Thordric breathed. 'In my head; there were no words, but I could understand it all the same. It was screaming for everything coming in from Fyoras to get out.' He slouched down against the side of the ship, coming to rest on the floor.

'But how could that hurt you?' Ourellus asked.

At the commotion, Hamlet had come out of the cabin. When he saw his friend on the floor, so obviously in pain, he went even whiter than he was already. 'What happened to him?' he demanded of the others.

'We're not sure,' Kal said to him. 'One minute, Thordric reached out to touch one of those pillars, the next he was like this.'

'It sent out a pulse into my arm,' Thordric said, sitting up. 'At the same time, I heard this awful thing in my head. It was strong and angry. I don't think another species would have survived it, particularly not a smaller species. It felt like it wanted to kill me but was forbidden from doing so.'

Ourellus and Lyanis stared at him. 'Did you see an image of it in your mind?' Ourellus asked, a note of urgency in his voice.

'I...yes, I think so. But it looked like a flash of smoke,' he replied.

Lyanis's eyes widened. 'You don't think that he...?' she said to Ourellus.

'Unfortunately, I think that's exactly what he's done. Of all the idiotic things...!'

'What who's done?' Thordric asked them, fearing that he had done something terribly wrong.

'My brother,' Ourellus replied. 'One of the magics that we're out to collect, the one from Numteqa, to the west...has the side-power to control beasts and trap their life force inside objects. It's unsteady magic if it's used on its own, but in conjunction with the other three, it's quite easy to subdue. Mother and I think that Kalljard used this power to trap a beast that lives in the mountain ranges between Numteqa and Fyoras. Not many people have heard of it, and even less have seen one.'

Hamlet, who had been kneeling on the floor next to Thordric, stood up, panic etched in every line on his face. 'If you're on about what I think you are, then this is bad, *very* bad,' he said, swallowing. He turned to Thordric and Kal, who were waiting impatiently for an explanation. 'The creature that we're talking about doesn't really have much of a physical body. It resembles a cloud, or a strange kind of smoke most of the time. The only reason I even know they exist is because one of my friends from university found traces of the minerals in their bodies inside a piece of rock that was rumoured to come from the mountains. They're believed to be extinct now, as there's nothing else alive in those mountains for them to feed on. Their bodies are made of a substance that, when touched, will eat away at its enemies. If Kalljard used his magic to put them into these pillars, then the reason that no creatures come across the border is because they'll be slain if they do.'

'Though I believe he commanded them not to touch humans and species similar to them,' Ourellus said. 'Otherwise, we would all be dead by now. I think the reason why it hurt you when you touched the pillar is because it couldn't resist attacking something so physically close to it. The danger, though, is that these creatures are possibly strong enough to break free if the spell on them is not restored every ten years.'

Everyone looked at each other. They had no idea when Kalljard might have last strengthened the spell, and even if he'd done it the year he died, six years had already passed, leaving only four more.

Thordric felt weak. 'I suppose we just have to hurry.' He scrambled over to where he kept the maps and unravelled the one of Fyoras. 'There's a small town about half a day from here. We can stop there and stock up on our food and water, then go straight on and find...' he looked at Lyanis, realising that he had no idea what the form of magic they needed there was.

'It's actually a type of herb, kept at the palace in the royal city. Only those of royal blood are allowed to eat it, which is why they keep it under heavy protection. Or at least they did,' she corrected herself, making Thordric consider how much time had passed since she'd last been there.

'So, I have to try and convince them to give me some?' he said, wondering what he could possibly do to satisfy them. He doubted that fixing a leak in the roof with his magic or something else so trivial would do the trick.

'That's the idea, yes. If the people here are still how I remember, then I don't think you'll have a problem.'

For some reason, her words made him more nervous than ever.

They reached the town Thordric had seen on the map before noon the next day. As they lowered the ship close enough to the ground to put the ladder down, a crowd of people rushed out of the small stone buildings nearby, gazing up at it.

Most of them were wearing clothes made of thin linen, wrapped around like togas. Thordric noticed that they were nearly all women, with only three or four men present, two of them old and frail.

As they disembarked, the people from the town seemed to realise that apart from Lyanis, Thordric and the others were all men, for they were pointing at them and muttering excitedly.

'What's going on?' Thordric whispered to Ourellus, as

some of the younger women came up to him and started pulling at his robes and touching his face, making him blush.

Ourellus was having the same thing done to him, as were Kal and Hamlet, who had both flushed deeper than the sunburn on Thordric's nose. 'I'm not sure,' he whispered back. 'Mother, do you know?'

Lyanis was standing to the side, watching as the women took turns coming up to see them. 'I believe they're seeing if you're all suitable as husband material,' she said with a smirk.

'What?' they cried unanimously.

She laughed. 'For some reason, most of the children born in this country are female, meaning that men are quite a rarity here. Those that do manage to find husbands have as many children as they can in the hopes that they will give birth to more boys. I wasn't sure if it was still a problem, so I didn't think to mention it, but obviously it is.'

'How do we get them to stop?' Hamlet pleaded, as two women started grabbing at his sleeves, feeling for muscle but only finding skinny arms.

In answer, Lyanis stepped forwards and spoke to an elderly woman dressed in darker clothing than the others. The language she used was soft and lyrical, like the sound of a flowing stream. The older woman replied to her, and then spoke out to the crowd, who edged back from them rather sulkily.

'What did you say to her?' Thordric asked curiously, as the crowd started to filter away into the town.

'I told her that we were here to get provisions before heading to the royal city. I asked her to tell the others to kindly wait until we've completed our journey to discuss who you will be married off to.'

'What did you do that for?' he spluttered, flushing pink again.

'I had to think of a reason for them to let us take some of their food and water and pass through. They've also agreed to let us bathe,' she added, chuckling as they suddenly all agreed what a wonderful plan it had been.

They followed the elderly woman through the town to a large, stone hall, which to their delight, had two enormous baths the size of swimming pools. They had the water all to themselves, as Lyanis had made the old woman, who was the town's elder, swear not to let anyone else in. Lyanis herself, noticing how uncomfortable the others were about the idea of sharing the baths with her, chose to wait until they were finished to bathe herself.

Dirt free and with their clothes thoroughly washed by the women of the town (who had used a scented washing powder made from sweet berries so that each garment carried a soft perfume), they restocked *Dinia's Jewel* with plenty of fresh food and water, ready for their departure. The elder also gave them a small, hand drawn map of the royal city, as there was a maze at the entrance to stop any thieves wishing to steal the royal family's herb.

They thanked her and the townspeople, but didn't linger any more than they had to, and soon they were off again, flying across the town and over the countryside beyond. Unlike the burning desert they'd crossed, Fyoras was pleasantly warm aside from the hours when the sun was at its highest.

The royal city was located right in the heart of the country, on a small island surrounded by a short stretch of water. It was built from a different type of stone than the towns they had flown across, and in the sunlight, it shimmered like mother-of-pearl.

It was so tightly packed together that there was no place to land the ship inside, and as the walls reached to the very edge of the island that it was built on, their only choice was to land *Dinia's Jewel* on the far side of the water. They disembarked in front of the single bridge leading across to the large gates of the city.

Taking only the provisions they could carry and making sure that they had the map of the city's inner maze with them, they crossed the bridge – if, in fact, they could even call it that. It was made of a single piece of thick rope and had two guide ropes either side of it at shoulder height, which they could cling to in order to stop themselves falling into the water.

It took every ounce of concentration they had for them to cross without getting wet, even for Lyanis, who was considerably lighter footed than the others, and when they finally got to the other side, they found two female guards standing in front of the gate, armed with long steel spears. However, the guards made no move as the party went past them, except to eye up the men with great interest. Thordric felt a shiver go up his spine as they did so and hurried on as quickly as he could.

The doors led straight into the maze as the map had shown them. Its walls were sixty feet high and were covered in a blanket of orange and pink flowers. Hamlet made to sniff them, but Lyanis pulled him back sharply.

'I wouldn't do that if I were you. The scent of those flowers is enough to put you to sleep for a week,' she said, shaking her head. 'Honestly, how much security do they need?'

Thordric had been wondering the same thing, but then it occurred to him that people from other countries still travelled here and probably knew about the powers of the herb the same as they did. He wondered if he would see anyone from lands beyond the ones surrounding Dinia, for there was no information on them at all, except for the knowledge that they existed. Exactly how many there were and how big each country was, no one in Dinia knew – or at least, no one still living.

They turned a corner, going the way the map dictated, discovering yet more flowers lining the walls. Thordric eyed the ground and saw that several small creatures were wrapped up in vines extending down from the flowers. He gulped and glanced at Lyanis.

'As well as putting people to sleep, these plants aren't carnivorous, are they?' he asked nervously.

'There are no carnivorous plants in this country; they all grow in Numteqa. If you look closely, you'll see that those creatures are awake. They're the only ones who can withstand the flower's scent, and so they like to nest in it,' she said reassuringly.

He took a closer look as she'd suggested, noticing that the creatures were moving slightly. They had thin, furry bodies with four legs and a long snout, with green leathery wings sprouting from their backs.

'What are they?' he asked, thinking that they actually looked quite lovable.

'I believe they're called Miets. They may look adorable,' she said, noticing how he was admiring them, 'but they can be very aggressive when they want to be. I'd stay away from them, myself.'

He sighed and moved on with the rest of the group, following the twists and turns on the map and completely losing his sense of direction.

12

THE WILTING HERB

They had been in the maze for hours, following the route on the map religiously so that they didn't take any wrong turns. However, by this time, Thordric was seriously starting to doubt the map's accuracy.

'Shouldn't we have found our way out of here by now?' he asked Lyanis, who was now the only one keeping pace. The others, though not having sniffed the flowers growing on the walls directly, were feeling the effects of their scent as it wafted towards them as they passed. Hamlet seemed to be suffering the most, yawning so often that Thordric thought he might collapse with weariness at any moment. He had a feeling that it was because Hamlet didn't possess any magic, as Kal and Ourellus (who, despite being rusty with his powers, was still radiating with magic) had only recently started dragging their feet.

Thordric himself was fine, but then again, he could feel the magic of the Criads' sacred antlers inside him, pulsing as though actively dispelling the poisonous aroma.

Lyanis simply shrugged. The scent wasn't affecting her at

all, though he supposed it was because of her abilities as a forest dweller, which hadn't failed to surprise him yet. 'I don't know. The maze wasn't here last time I came,' she said. Her brow creased slightly. 'If I remember correctly, the royal city was less than half the size it is now, and it certainly wasn't on an island. Yet I suppose I shouldn't be surprised. A thousand years is ample time for a country to develop.'

'Then you have no idea if the map they gave us has the right path on it?' he asked in a pained voice.

'It must be. I doubt that they would deliberately give us the wrong path with what I promised. The idea is too valuable to them.'

Thordric's insides squirmed guiltily. There was no way they could possibly fulfil the promise they had given the women in the village; no one was in any position for marriage yet. 'I have to find out,' he decided. 'Do you feel like having a look?'

'And how do you suppose I do that?' she asked archly, staring up at the sixty-foot walls.

Instead of replying, Thordric used his magic to levitate her all the way up to the top. Even this, which by far was the magic he was best at, was now so remarkably easy it felt he wasn't doing anything at all.

'What can you see?' he shouted, unsure if she could hear him, for by the way her long hair was whipping about her, the wind above them was very strong. She wailed in reply and Thordric put her down hastily.

As she touched the ground, he couldn't help laughing. Her thin clothes had been blown all out of place and her hair hung in bushy clumps around her face. He even thought he saw that her cheeks, usually silvery grey like the rest of her skin, had a touch of pink to them.

She hit him.

'Ouch! What was that for?' he said, clutching his burning cheek.

'Warn me next time you plan to do something like that. I was terrified!' she snapped, straightening out her hair and clothes.

'Sorry,' he said. 'I didn't think you'd mind.'

'I may look like I'm your age, but just now I felt my years flash before me. All three hundred of them,' she added acidly.

Thordric stared at her. 'But you've been frozen for over a thousand years; you must be older than that,' he said, trying to work it out on his fingers.

She hit him again, though this time it wasn't as hard. 'Fine then, *one thousand* and three hundred,' she said, and turned away from him to march around the next corner.

He made a mental note not to bring up her age again, or to use any magic on her without her permission. Ourellus and Kal both shook their heads at him, now dragging a dozing Hamlet along between them.

'You'd better go after her and ask what she saw up there. I don't fancy walking around here for another half a day simply because you upset her,' Kal said, wiping sweat from under his dreadlocks.

Thordric did so and dashed around the corner, but she wasn't there. Instead of another pathway, the walls had opened out into a wide archway, and beyond it was one of the busiest streets he'd ever seen. There were hundreds of stalls lining both sides of it, selling hot curried food, spices, fruits, vegetables, nuts, various types of clothing, jewellery, and rugs. In the distance, he could hear a band playing hand drums and some type of reed instrument. He'd never known a place as bright and full of life as this; not even Neathin Valley, which, with all its brightly coloured houses and peculiarly dressed people, was saying something.

Like the town they had been to, the people were mostly women, but there were a few more men about than before. Everyone was dressed in rich colours, ranging from deep, burnt orange to vibrant purple. It was like looking out at a school of fish, darting about this way and that, reflecting the sunlight on their scales.

'Where's mother?' Ourellus asked, his eyes too dazzled to think straight.

Thordric blinked. He had completely forgotten that she was missing. They went through the archway into the street itself, and immediately women from all sides started accosting them again, though this time it was because they were trying to sell them things. 'I'm sorry, I don't have any money,' Thordric said, as one particularly forceful woman tried to wrap a large silk scarf around his neck, putting her hand in his pocket at the same time and pulling out a small bronze penny, stamped with the Wizard Council's symbol. She looked at it in disgust before throwing it onto the floor, almost strangling him as she pulled the scarf back off, muttering words he couldn't understand.

He turned around and saw that Hamlet, still half asleep, was being dragged over to one of the food stalls selling potent curry. The girl leading him took a small spoonful of red powder and poured it onto his tongue. The effect was instantaneous. He jumped up, his pale complexion turning bright red, and his eyes watering so much it looked like he was crying. He grabbed at his throat, trying to say something, but no words came out. The girl seemed confused, obviously never having seen a reaction like this, and tried to shoo him away to stop him upsetting the large bowls of curry on her stall.

Thordric steered him away quickly and pulled off the water flask he was wearing over his shoulder, unscrewing the cap and pouring the whole lot down Hamlet's throat. 'Thanks,' Hamlet gasped, the redness draining from his face. 'I don't know what happened. One minute Kal was holding me as he looked at one of the other stalls – there's really unusual pottery over there, you know – and then before I knew it, she got hold of me and gave me that...whatever it was.'

'I think it's chilli,' Kal said, coming over and sniffing the air. 'They grow one like it in a town between Jard Town and Neathin Valley, though I doubt it's anywhere near as strong. Captain Jal, my foster father, occasionally stopped off there to bring some back with him on *The Jardine*. I tried some once, it was d—'

'I'm sure it's nice for you all to stand around and talk, but we really must get to the palace,' Lyanis said, appearing behind them and looking as jostled as they were. She noticed how they were all staring at her, and said, 'A group of women saw me as I went through the archway and took me to be fitted into one of their ridiculous dresses.'

Kal sniggered and Lyanis shot him a poisonous look, silencing him immediately.

The path to the palace was blissfully straight. There was only one turn at the end of the main street, which broke out into several acres of fields full of crops, and the palace stood behind them, accessible by a small footpath almost hidden from view.

Instead of the sharp angular architecture of the main town, the palace was completely dome shaped and built out of the same mother-of-pearl-coloured stone that made up the walls of the maze. As they made their way up to the main door, which was also round, a plump woman with expertly plaited hair came out to meet them.

They looked at her in surprise, for she seemed to be specifically waiting for them. 'Did they know we were coming?' Thordric asked Lyanis.

'I suspect so. One of the powers of the herb we need is that it grants the eater the power of foresight,' she explained as they reached the woman.

'Foresight? You mean looking into the future?' Kal said in wonder. 'I didn't think that was possible. I know there are some people that claim to do it, but I thought they were all fakes.'

'They probably are,' Lyanis said. 'No form of magic that I know of can make it possible other than this herb.'

'If it can do that,' Hamlet asked shrewdly, 'then why didn't Kalljard see his death coming?'

'I doubt he figured out how to do it, or at least, if he did, he would not have wanted to use it. My son lived in the present and did not like to dwell on the future other than to plan his ascension over the country. Still, if he had have done, then perhaps he would have realised what a huge mistake he was making,' she replied. She turned to the woman waiting for them, who was watching with a smile.

'Welcome to the Royal Palace of Fyoras,' she said in perfect Dinian. 'Their highnesses await you in the throne room. I am Ilka, and if you follow me, I shall take you to them.'

She turned and led them through the round door into the circular, open halls of the palace, which were decorated with carvings of flowers and animals, and a plant motive that repeated all the way around the wall. A large, curved staircase came down from the centre of the ceiling, also decorated with the plant motif, and she took them to the top where it opened out into another large hall, even more elaborately decorated. Children, both boys and girls, ran around playing and calling to each other, with circlets of mother-of-pearl decorating their heads. At one end of the hall were two thrones carved from white marble and sitting in them were a man and woman dressed in robes of pure silver thread. The man wore a matching turban, but the woman wore a circlet like the children, only much larger.

Ilka stopped in front of them and turned. 'May I introduce their highnesses King Pedante and Queen Kriisha of Fyoras.' She bowed low and the others copied her, all a little awkwardly except for Lyanis, who curtsied gracefully.

'So, you are the wizards from Dinia,' King Pedante said, standing up. His queen joined him and together they walked towards them.

'Yes, your highness,' Ourellus said, but the King looked past him at Thordric.

'You not only possess your own magic, but also that of the sacred antlers of the Criads, do you not?' he asked.

Thordric coughed, surprised. 'Yes, your highness. How did you know?'

'The herb gives us much knowledge; I can feel a power in you that is not your own. Tell me, why is it that you wish to gather the magics of Fyoras, Uoo, Numteqa and Wyotis when your own is already so strong?' he asked. It was not an accusation, but simple curiosity.

'Because my magic, even though you say it's strong, isn't powerful enough to help free my friend,' Thordric said, a sharp pang at the image of Vey's frozen face splintering up his spine.

'You refer to the current High Wizard?' Queen Kriisha said, her speech much more accented than her husband's.

'I do. His name's Vey.'

The Queen laid a hand on his shoulder, and a warmth flowed into him that was not unlike the one coming from the sacred antlers. It made him feel much better. 'We understand your plight,' she continued. 'But I am afraid we cannot help you, for you see...the herb is dying, and we have no way of remedying it.'

Lyanis gasped. 'What do you mean, it's dying? That's impossible!'

'I'm afraid it is true,' the King said. 'You may look for yourself if you wish, forest dweller, yet I doubt if even you can help it.'

'Take me to it,' she said at once.

The King and Queen looked at each other, engaging in some kind of unspoken agreement. 'We shall,' the King said, and swept past her and down the spiral staircase into the hall below. They watched as he pressed a button, hidden on one of the motifs carved into the wall, and a panel opened in the floor to reveal a straight stone staircase leading down under the room.

It only took them a few minutes to reach the bottom. The chamber it came out in was square and plain, with simple sconces in each corner. In the centre was a large patch of earth, and planted in it was what resembled a small, sickly looking weed.

'No!' Lyanis cried when she saw it, kneeling to the ground for a better look. 'What have you done to it?'

She touched it gently, and a withered leaf dropped off it. She picked the leaf up and examined it, worry etched across her face.

'We have only cared for it as our family has always done,' the Queen said. 'There are no records of it ever being like this, though. We simply do not know what to do.'

'This ground,' Lyanis asked. 'Has it been disturbed lately?'

'No, we have not touched it, save from watering,' the Queen replied.

'And have you avoided picking it on a full moon?'

'I...no, there is nothing about that in the instructions left by our ancestors,' the King said, frowning.

'Oh, the fools. I told them last time that if they kept on

doing it, it would lose its power to sustain itself over the years.' She looked at the King and Queen seriously. 'The moon has a great effect on how this herb grows. Even though it does not need natural light, the power of the moon still reaches it here. A full moon is when it depends on it the most, and if it is picked at that time, it does not regenerate properly.'

The King and Queen turned ashen. 'So, there is really nothing we can do?'

'No, there is something, and I must say that your luck is certainly strong. I believe that the magic of Dinia, enhanced by the sacred antlers, can restore it enough to help it replenish itself.'

Everyone looked at Thordric. He gulped.

13

BATTLE OF INNER MAGIC

L yanis explained in depth what was wrong with the herb so Thordric could restore it back to its full vigour. She told him that the cells storing the plant's regenerative powers had collapsed due to being cut at the wrong time, and all he had to do was rebuild the cell walls so that they were stable again.

Thordric was no expert in the biology of plants; even when he made potions, the only thing he had to know about them was what magical properties they had. The idea of trying to get to grips with the herb's very make-up made him less than confident, but she seemed to think it would be easy for him.

'Plants are like any other species,' she said. 'If they're healthy, they thrive. If they're not, then they become weak and die. Be careful, though. If you fortify the cells too much, it might have the reverse effect and make the herb unstable. Remember, this is a very special plant, and there's not another like it in the world.'

She smiled, believing her words would encourage him, but all Thordric felt was a tightness in his stomach at the thought of failing. If he couldn't save the herb, then he might not be able to rescue Vey, even if he obtained the two remaining magics.

Everyone gathered around to watch him work. He tried to relax and focus his mind, reaching out to the herb and searching for its life force, but he could hear everyone taking deep breaths, waiting for something to happen. His hands grew clammy.

Trying again, he managed to grasp the tip of its life force. Then the King whispered something to his Queen, jarring his concentration, and he lost it again. He swallowed and wiped his already wet brow. 'I...don't suppose you could wait in the other room, could you?' he asked, turning to them all.

'Oh,' Queen Kriisha said, straightening herself. She had been leaning in closely, attempting to figure out what he was doing. 'If we are distracting you...then I suppose we can withdraw and let you work alone.'

She led the others out of the room, obviously disappointed, and shut the panel at the top of the staircase as she went, leaving Thordric alone. He let out a long breath, stretching to rid himself of the tension that'd built up in his shoulders. This time when he focused, he managed to grasp the herb's life force easily, and following it back to its core, located the regenerative cells Lyanis had told him about. He knew they were the right ones, for all the other cells were perfectly fine – aside from feeling a bit withered.

The walls of the regenerative cells had indeed collapsed, almost as if they'd been made of brick and someone had given them a few good blows with a hammer. As he examined them with his magic, the power of the sacred antlers hummed inside him. It seemed like their power was trying to tell him something. Curious, he closed his eyes and let the feeling travel up into his mind. He saw something; the cell walls were closing up, almost as if they were being sewn together. They were stabilizing.

Opening his eyes, he reached out to the plant once more, thinking about his vision. No sooner had he done so than the power of the sacred antlers took over. It flowed from him as though he were a cup overfilled with water and, before he knew it, the images he'd seen in his head were happening for real. The cell walls were being sewn up, and the plant was regaining its health.

He watched as the stem and leaves straightened up, becoming a rich green, and a delicate white flower began to bloom. The petals glowed like moonlight on a clear night, far outshining the fire in the sconces on the walls. It was beautiful.

A grinding came from the ceiling, and the panel above the staircase opened. 'Thordric, are you alright down there?' Hamlet called down to him.

Thordric laughed, the relief of having healed the herb spreading through him so quickly that his legs became weak, and he had to sit on the floor. 'Yes, I think you should come down here,' he replied happily.

There was a sound like someone falling down the stairs, and Hamlet appeared in the room. Thordric looked at him, noticing that he was nursing his elbow. 'Missed the step,' Hamlet said, wincing. 'How are you getting—'

He stopped, his eyes widening as he saw the fully restored herb. 'You did it!' he gasped, running over to it. 'I've never seen anything like it, not even in the fossil records at the University. No wonder they take their security seriously here. The Queen wasn't sure if you could do it, she thought it was too late, you see, but...wow! Really, this is...'

Thordric grinned as Hamlet knelt beside him, marvelling at the herb's radiance. Rummaging inside his pockets, Thordric pulled out a vial of the orange potion that reduced swelling and gave it to him to rub on his elbow. Hamlet applied it gratefully, feeling the bump go down quickly.

Then they heard footsteps coming down the stairs, and a moment later, the others appeared. The Queen shrieked as soon as she saw the herb, throwing her arms around the King and kissing him deeply in celebration. Thordric, Hamlet and Kal all looked away, but Lyanis and Ourellus were smiling broadly.

'I told you he could do it, didn't I?' Lyanis said airily to the Queen once her highness's lips were unglued from the King's mouth again.

'And to think I did not believe it,' the Queen said. She went over to Thordric and helped him up off the floor, cupping his face in her hands. He thought at first that she was going to kiss him too, but instead she said, 'Not only will we give you a cup full of the herb's petals, but we shall also give you the hand of any maiden you desire in the palace. My handmaidens are particularly lovely; one of them is about your age, I believe—'

He squirmed out of her grasp, blushing profusely. 'No, thank you,' he spluttered. 'It's a very kind offer, but with my duties at the Wizard Council, I'm afraid I have to refuse.'

Ourellus, Hamlet and Lyanis all smiled at him, but it was far too much for Kal. He fell about the floor, laughing openly at Thordric's increasingly crimson face. Thordric scowled and levitated him upside down, making his dreadlocks dangle like a mop.

'You are sure?' the Queen said, watching Kal zoom back and forth, with his head grazing the floor. 'After all, we have so few men in our country; it would be nice to have some more.'

Thordric finally let Kal back down. He hit the floor with a thump and sat up, nursing his head. Thordric threw him some orange potion and then turned back to the Queen. 'I'm sure, thank you, your highness,' he said to her.

She sighed and looked at the others. 'Perhaps your friends would be interested?' she asked, eyeing the men up. They all avoided her gaze. 'Then I suppose I must accept your decision,' she said. She looked at the King, who caught her eyes and pulled a pair of tiny, golden shears from one of the folds in his turban. He handed them to Thordric along with a mother-of-pearl lined cup.

'You may cut the brightest petals for yourself. Keep them in that cup and seal it with the lid until midnight. Only then can you eat them to get their full power,' he said.

Thordric did so, clipping enough petals to fill the cup completely. He turned and gave the shears back. 'Thank you,' he said. 'Without this, we wouldn't be able to save High Wizard Vey.'

'No, we are the ones who must thank you. The herb would surely have died if you hadn't saved it, and our people would suffer without it. Though only members of the royal family may consume it, we use the powers it gives us to ensure that the crops always grow strong and plentiful regardless of the heat and make fresh springs available to all the towns in our country,' he replied, shaking Thordric's hand.

'I hear you are now headed to Numteqa,' the Queen said, embracing her husband as he spoke. Thordric looked blankly at Lyanis, who nodded encouragingly. Apparently, she'd already decided.

'It seems that we are,' he said.

'Then we shall send you with an escort out of the city,' the Queen said, an amused lilt to her voice.

Good to her word, the Queen sent a young girl from the palace to take them back through the town, away from all the people still mingling about the stalls. Instead of leading them back through the maze, however, she went over to one of the walls past the archway and pulled back part of the curtain of flowers.

'Don't touch those,' Hamlet cried out in alarm, but she laughed at him, saying something to Lyanis in the soft language of Fyoras.

'She says not to worry, the flowers on this part are all fake. They will not harm her,' Lyanis translated.

The girl was obviously telling the truth, for behind the curtain of fake flowers was a small doorway. She opened it and beckoned them to go through into a cramped, dark room.

They found themselves facing a narrow ladder, which she deftly climbed up, gesturing for them to follow. After a strenuous climb, she called for them to stop. She stretched out her hand to open a stone panel above her head. They went through the gap, finding themselves on top of the wall.

'Oh, gosh, I've ended up back here again,' said Lyanis, glancing down at the ground far below. Her silvery hue drained away, leaving her skin grey.

'So, it's heights you're afraid of?' Thordric asked her. 'Then why were you alright on *Dinia's Jewel* and when we rode on the Criads' backs?'

She looked at him, going greyer still. 'I had something to hold on to then. Now there's nothing.'

'Don't be silly, mother,' Ourellus said beside her. He held out his hand to her, and Thordric, catching on, did the same. Kal and Hamlet joined in too, and they formed a long chain, each depending on the balance of the others.

Like this, they followed the girl along the tops of the walls until they reached the other side, where she opened another panel and led them back down to the ground, right in front of the city's gates. She bowed low and then darted off back up to the top of the wall. They watched her disappear out of sight before going through the gates and across the single rope bridge to *Dinia's Jewel*.

Now that their journey was half complete, they all felt a little better. Once they had the magic from Numteqa, they could fly straight on down to Wyotis. After they'd gathered the magic from there, they could free Vey.

At midnight that night, as the King had instructed, Thordric opened the cup full of herb petals. They shone even brighter outside and, one by one, he ate them, feeling a peculiar sensation in his stomach as though he'd swallowed a lot of water very quickly. It made him feel ill and tired, so he laid down and wrapped himself in blankets. After no more than a few minutes, he fell deeply asleep.

In the morning, to the sound of Kal and Ourellus cooking eggs over a magical fire, he woke to find that the sun was blooming across the horizon.

'You're finally awake,' Kal said, not looking up as he flipped the eggs in the pan. 'We were going to wake you up yesterday, but Lyanis said to let you sleep.'

'Yesterday?' Thordric said, yawning. 'But I only went to sleep last night.'

'No, you've been asleep for nearly three days. We're back in Dinia now,' Ourellus said, but then stopped, his mouth hanging open. 'Your eyes! They're glowing!' he exclaimed, shaking Kal so that he looked up from his eggs to stare too.

Thordric fought off his blankets and searched through one of their bags for a mirror. Pulling one out, he took in his reflection. It was true, his eyes *were* glowing. It was the same luminescence the herb petals had.

'It'll wear off in a few days,' Lyanis said calmly, resting her hand gently on the ship's wheel as she watched him. 'It takes a while for the herb's magic to be fully absorbed by your body, so until then, it tries to leak out,' she continued.

She asked Ourellus to take the wheel and went over to Thordric to check him. 'How do you feel otherwise?' she asked, holding his head in her delicate hands, and examining him thoroughly.

'Fine,' he said. 'Though it feels as though the magic of the sacred antlers and the herb's magic are repelling each other at the moment.'

'Hmm,' she said, pursing her lips. 'It didn't occur to me that that might happen. When I gave the four magics to Kalljard as an infant, they all went into his body at the same time. Perhaps the other two magics will help them merge a bit more. Until then, though, maybe you can see if you can harness some of the herb's magic anyway.'

He spent the rest of the day trying to do exactly that, though the magic of the sacred antlers seemed to block the herb's magic every time he tried. Eventually, he gave up attempting to use it separately and concentrated on using his magic normally, hoping that the herb's magic would simply join in. The spell he was trying to do was to further enhance the potion running the ship so that it would take them even less time to get to Numteqa. That had been Ourellus's idea, after Hamlet had told him about the time Vey had done it to all the ships in the fleet of the floating Ships of Kal.

Thordric had no idea what method Vey had used at the time, so he'd tried to figure it out on his own. He'd settled on strengthening the effects of the individual herbs in the potion and seeing what happened after that, but where his magic had become so easy after he'd been given the sacred antlers, it was now even more difficult than it had been with just his normal abilities.

Despite his efforts not to use it, the magic of the antlers

pushed through anyway, and it did it so forcefully that his focus was pushed off the potion fuelling the ship and onto the wood behind it, which erupted in a rash of newly sprouted branches, despite the heavy magical varnish painted over the entire deck.

'For Spell's sake, butt out of it!' he cried out loud, making everyone look around with concern. To his surprise, though, it worked. The magic became subdued and shunted aside, enough to let the magic of the herb leak through. He tried the spell again, going through it slowly and encouraging the herb's magic out with all his might.

The potion running the ship swiftly changed colour, and with a lurch, the ship began speeding faster through the sky, so that everyone had to hold on tightly to avoid skidding back into the cabin.

Finally, he'd managed to control the herb's magic at last! Yet as he sat down to enjoy some well-deserved dinner, he could have sworn that he felt the magic of the sacred antlers grumbling about inside him. He shrugged and squashed it down with a plateful of sausages, talking with the others about the best path to Numteqa.

14

RETURN OF THE DRUNKEN MAN

Thordric knocked on the door of Mr Henders' house and waited, holding his cloak tightly about him as a chill wind swept down the street.

Mr Henders was a half-wizard who lived in Valley Edge, and he and Thordric had met three years ago when Thordric had travelled to Neathin Valley on business for the Wizard Council. He had a brother called Grale who used to live in the mountains between Dinia and Numteqa, and it was for that very reason Thordric was there now.

Mr Henders opened the door, surprise in every line on his face. 'My, my, I didn't expect to see you here, Thordric,' he said, standing to the side to let him in. Thordric wiped his feet and made his way into the lounge.

The decor hadn't changed since Thordric had been there last; the room was full of hats of various shapes and sizes, most of which Mr Henders sold at the market down by the docks where *The Jardine* came in.

'So, what can I do for you?' Mr Henders said, offering Thordric some tea and biscuits that he'd summoned from his kitchen. Thordric smiled; Mr Henders' control over his magic had greatly improved now that he'd received some training from the council. Thordric remembered when he had been scared to use it because of an accident that happened as a child, leaving him with a bent spine and a clawed hand. Vey had managed to heal them for him and encouraged Mr Henders to take lessons so that he no longer had to be afraid.

'Actually,' Thordric said, helping himself to tea, 'I wondered if Grale still lived here with you.'

'Grale? Yes, he's upstairs now, I believe. He did move out for a while, but the landlady threw him out recently because he refused to fix a window that he broke when he was in a temper.' Mr Henders spoke mildly, but if Thordric knew Grale, then it had probably been quite the incident. 'What do you need him for if I may ask?'

Knowing he could trust him, Thordric told Mr Henders about Vey's situation and their journey to gather the four magics from the surrounding countries. 'We're heading to Numteqa next, but the only way to get there is across the mountains. We could fly there, but I heard they regularly get snowstorms. Grale is the only person I know who's been up there before, so I wanted to ask if he'd guide us.'

'I remember Grale's stories about the mountains. The border goes right across them, I believe, so he met many Numteqians up there. That's where he managed to get all that alcohol,' Mr Henders said, disapprovingly.

'Did I hear someone talking about Numteqa?' Grale said, looming in the doorway. He was slightly stockier than Mr Henders, and compared to Mr Henders' well-groomed nature, he looked scraggly and unkempt. 'Well, Spell me,' he said, seeing Thordric. 'What are you doing here? There's not another disaster going on, is there?'

He eyed Thordric suspiciously, remembering only too well the giant forest that had overtaken the town when Thordric had been there last, caused by a mix of ancient and modern magic that Thordric and Vey had sorted out with the help of Hamlet.

'No, it's nothing like that,' Thordric reassured him. 'I need to get across the mountains to Numteqa.'

'That sounds awfully daring for someone of the council,' Grale replied. 'Why do you need to go?'

'There's some magic in Numteqa that I need to get. Vey's been trapped by a frozen in time spell left by Kalljard. I need this magic to help free him.'

'The High Wizard's frozen? I bet that upset the old fogies at the council,' Grale sneered, his distaste for the older Council members, who had been there under Kalljard's rule, failing to keep from his lips. 'Who's in charge at the moment, with Vey like that and you here?'

'Vey's mother,' Thordric said, sipping his tea. 'She might not have any magic, but she's tough enough to keep them all in line.' He blinked, realising that he hadn't spoken to her since they'd left. He should check up and see if she really was managing alright.

Grale laughed. 'Well, as long as it's not one of those old fools. There'd be nothing left of it by the time you got back.' He considered the situation. 'I suppose if you're going up the mountains, you'll want me to guide you.'

'If it's not too much trouble,' Thordric said.

Grale shook his head. 'No, I like it up there. Less people, see. It'd also be a good opportunity to stock up on my whisky supply.'

Mr Henders made a strained sort of cough.

'I was only joking, brother. Don't unravel your hat ribbons,' Grale said, rolling his eyes. He turned back to Thordric. 'How are we getting to the mountains? They're a fair way from here, and I don't feel like walking it again.'

'We've got the small floating ship from *The Jardine*,' Thordric said. 'It might be a bit cramped, but it'll get us there quickly.'

'Good. When do we leave?' Grale asked.

Dinia's Jewel sped across the countryside, heading west. What would have taken them a week's journey by carriage only took them a few hours now that Thordric had made the ship faster.

Grale spent most of it mooning over Lyanis, much to Ourellus's annoyance. In fact, Ourellus had been so put out by him that he'd accidentally steered the ship into a rain cloud and got them all wet, leading to several waspish complaints. Sensing the tension, Kal and Hamlet had gone into the cabin to read up about the creatures in Numteqa and to prepare their warm clothing for when they disembarked at the base of the mountains. Thordric wished he'd gone with them, for the tension between Ourellus and Grale got so strong that Thordric told them to stay at separate sides of the ship while he took the wheel himself. He also sternly told Lyanis not to flirt with anyone else.

'I don't understand why he has a problem with it,' she scoffed. 'I may be his mother, but why should that mean that I can't have some fun sometimes? It's not like I want to start any serious relationships.'

'I'm sure he just feels protective of you. I mean, you *do* look young and naive, and you've been frozen in time for so long that the world's completely changed,' Thordric replied.

'May I remind you that he was frozen too? Twice, in fact,' she said.

'Yes, and look what happened. When he was revived the

first time, he met my mother and fell in love with her. Then Kalljard froze him again before he even realized she was pregnant with me. I never knew anything about him until now, all because he was careless with himself!' he snapped, suddenly angry. He hadn't intended to shout at her, but he knew what he was saying was true, and that Ourellus probably was being protective of her because he didn't want her to do anything as foolish as he'd done.

Lyanis fell silent. She glanced over Thordric's shoulder to where Ourellus stood, looking over the ship's side at the ground speeding past below and pretending not to have heard. She knew better, his hearing was as good as hers, and the conversation had hardly been quiet.

'You're right. I suppose I should behave myself,' she said, and with that, she too went into the cabin.

Thordric was surprised to find tears on his cheeks. He wiped them away quickly, feeling both Ourellus and Grale's eyes on him. He took a deep breath, and for the rest of the journey, spoke to Lizzie on his long-distance communicator.

According to her, the council was running smoothly, and there had been relatively little for the wizards to argue with her about. The one time that Wizard Ayek and his friends had kicked up a fuss was when she'd caught them terrorising some of the half-wizard students at the Training Facility, but Wizard Batsu, Thordric's friend, had used his magic to bar them from the entrance at her command. After that, Ayek had contented himself with sulking in his room.

Lyanis came back on deck as he put the communicator away. 'I've been discussing things with Hamlet and Kal, and we've all agreed that we need to head to Numteqa's south. There are small creatures called Ugamba, a type of rat with silver fur, that live there. Their fur is tougher than even diamond, so they're highly sought after by the people of

Numteqa, who desire to weave the fur into armoured shirts. Fortunately for the Ugamba, the strength of their fur makes them near impossible to slay, and they also have teeth laced with venom that will kill you in an instant. It's that very venom you need. Once it's distilled, its magical properties are almost as strong as the sacred antlers and the herb petals put together,' she explained.

Thordric gulped. 'Is there a safe way to get it?' he asked, feeling his voice quiver.

'The key is to trap one without hurting it. But I simply can't remember what method I used to actually extract the venom. And Thordric,' she said, 'this magic is probably the most important of the four, for not only will it help to free the High Wizard, but it's also the magic you need to restore the seal on the pillars along Dinia's border.'

Reaching the base of the mountain, they disembarked, clothed in thick, heavy robes treated with an insulating potion. Despite the howling gale that blew about them, they all remained warm and dry. Each of them carried a large pack on their backs, filled with water, food, blankets, and in Thordric's case, the map of Numteqa.

The mountain path was steep, and with snow billowing around them, it was hard to see where they were going. Grale instructed them to shout if they felt they were falling behind, but they managed to keep up with him until nightfall, where they reached the marker showing they were already a third of the way up.

They made camp among a cluster of large fir trees, and, with sudden insight, Thordric cast a large shielding spell over the entire area. Now getting used to both magics within him, he found that as long as he cast it strongly enough, it would remain for hours until he took it down. It kept the wind and snow out, so they were able to get a good fire going and were even lucky enough to catch a rabbit to roast.

Unfortunately, this offended Lyanis greatly, as she believed it was highly unnecessary to eat the flesh of another animal, only eating a mix of fruits, fungi, nuts, and vegetables herself. Thordric had tried to cheer her up by saying that it was an elderly rabbit that had been badly injured, but she simply turned her back on him and marched off into the trees inside the shield, digging for a plant known to grow there that had large, edible roots.

Rising early the next day, Grale took them down a side path, much smaller than the main one, which he said was a short cut. It was, but climbing it was almost like trying to climb a particularly sharp, rocky ladder, for the incline was so steep it was only a few degrees off from being completely vertical.

The path led them straight to the top, and they climbed well into the night in order to reach it by morning.

'It's no good, Thordric!' Hamlet shouted up from behind as Thordric took his last step, swinging his leg onto the outcrop a few feet away from the mountain's peak. 'I can't make it!'

Thordric turned around and saw that Hamlet was still a good thirty feet below, barely clinging onto the rock. The others had already reached the top and were resting a few feet away. 'Don't worry,' he shouted back. 'I'll levitate you the rest of the way. Hold on.'

He leant over the outcrop, getting a better look, and grasped Hamlet with his magic. He lifted him up slowly, but before he got him to the top, a powerful gust of wind knocked him over onto his back. Hamlet, who had been in mid-air at the time, found himself plummeting back down, where several large rocks protruded out from the mountainside.

Thordric sprang back up to his feet and lashed out again with his magic, catching Hamlet barely a second before he hit the rocks. He levitated Hamlet up and heaved him onto the comparative safety of the peak where the rest of the group were sitting. The two of them stared at each other, both wide eyed and pale.

'I think I need some tea,' Hamlet said at last, and Thordric managed a laugh.

'That's a very good idea,' he said, and produced a magical flame so they could boil some water.

They rested for another hour, while Grale trudged off to find the Numteqians that he had stayed with before. He wasn't going with them into Numteqa itself, so they needed a native to help them find their way down the mountains and to where the Ugamba lived.

He came back just as the wind started picking up again, followed by a man so hairy that at first, they though he was wearing animal furs. Instead, all the man wore was a knee length, sleeveless leather tunic and boots up to his calves. He carried with him only a light dagger, and with the thick beard covering most of his face, it was hard to make out what he was saying. It took everyone a moment to realise that he was speaking broken Dinian.

'This is Goras,' Grale said, introducing him. 'He'll help you down the mountains and is also familiar with the south of Numteqa. He was actually part of a hunting party trying capture one of the Ugamba, but, like everyone else, he failed.'

'Only one, in whole history, caught Ugamba before,' Goras said to them. 'A woman, say some, strange with silver skin, but beautiful.'

'Why, thank you,' Lyanis said, smiling at him in her usual way. Both Thordric and Ourellus cast her such disgusted looks that she stopped immediately.

'Impossible,' Goras said, her charm failing to work on him.

'It was before Goras's grandfather's grandfather was born. It could not have been you, young like that.'

'Looks can be deceiving,' she said sweetly. 'Anyway, I don't think we should linger here any longer. We need to move on.'

The pathway down the mountains was much more forgiving, and with Goras's guidance on how to tell where some areas of snow were deeper, it only took them a day. When they reached the bottom, they found a small village, built mostly from wooden logs, where they received a warm welcome at the inn. The innkeeper spared no time in giving them mugs of strong beer and nut laden pancakes, freshly cooked on the large stove heating the room.

Thordric and the others declined the beer at first, knowing full well that the ban on alcohol in Dinia was justified by the terrible clash it had with magic, but they soon found it was no use. Mugs were being pushed at them by everyone in the room, and when Hamlet, trying to calm them down, took his first sip, everyone cheered. However, far from leaving them alone, the villagers goaded them on even more, until finally, at well gone midnight, they all staggered to their rooms, vowing never to try drinking beer again, no matter how much the people wanted them to.

In the morning, Goras knocked loudly on their doors, causing great shouts of pain as a terrible ache hammered through everyone's heads. Lyanis, however, was unaffected, though they later found out that she'd only been pretending to drink, throwing the contents of her mug on the floor behind her as she mimicked taking long swigs.

The others took so long to recover that it was nearly noon by the time they set off again. Goras advised that trying to walk to where the Ugamba lived was unsafe and had bartered with the innkeeper to lease them some horses.

Thordric had been expecting an average, well-tempered thoroughbred, like Koleson, the horse he'd brought back with him from Neathin Valley, but the horses that Goras came back with made his jaw drop. They were each the size of a large carriage, with heavy builds and thick white coats. Their eyes were emerald-green, seeming to pierce right into Thordric's very being.

'Grosted horses,' Goras grunted when he asked about them. 'Bred to tread through deep snow. No better friend out in the wild here than a Grosted horse.'

They all clambered up on them, using high mounting blocks. It was odd being on a horse other than Koleson, especially one this large, but it was so calm and patient that Thordric bonded with it immediately. He patted its thick neck and headed out after the others, gazing across the land as the sun reflected brightly off the snow.

15

FANGS AND VENOM

Crossing the lake to reach the Ugamba's territory made Thordric uneasy, despite Goras reassuring them that the ice had never broken or melted in living history.

He could hear his horse's large hooves hitting the surface with a clack, even with the six inches or so of snow that was spread like a thick blanket over the entirety of it. He wondered if any creatures lived under it; perhaps a school of giant man-eating fish or a particularly dangerous type of water moss that would try to strangle them if they touched it. Neither would have surprised him, for as they'd already found out the previous evening, everything wild in Numteqa either tried to bite you or crush you to death – sometimes both.

It was only because of the Grosted horses that they'd managed to escape from being cornered by a pack of Vitas, a type of wolf with three legs – the single front one of which was twice the girth of the other two. Not only did the Vitas have long, razor sharp fangs and run extremely fast, but they were also infested with a plant called a Tangle Hold, which lived on the Vitas for the sole purpose of tangling around the legs of energetic prey and leaching its blood while the Vita ate the rest of the body.

Hamlet had seen one of the Vitas eating and observed this strange symbiotic relationship with awe – until the Tangle Hold lashed out, pulling him from his saddle into the freezing snow. Seconds later, twenty Vitas had formed a ring around the whole party. However, they hadn't been quick enough for Goras, who jumped off his horse and sliced the Tangle Hold's tentacles with his dagger, before helping Hamlet onto his horse and flipping acrobatically back onto his own.

The Grosted horses had snorted out a pale, yellow vapour, which confused the Vitas, and using the opportunity, they made their escape, galloping hard until there was no sign of the Vitas behind them at all.

As Thordric thought about the incident, he looked over at Hamlet, whose hands and fingers were still bandaged up with a special paste that removed any remaining bits of tangle hold from his skin. He'd been quiet and vague since it happened, not even taking an interest in the remains of an ancient village they'd passed through. There had been a carved stone obelisk in the centre, which he usually would have been fascinated by, but this time he'd barely glanced at it.

Deciding to see if he was alright, Thordric nudged his Grosted horse over to him. 'Hamlet?' he asked, louder than he'd intended.

Hamlet jumped violently, making his horse look around at him in surprise. 'Thordric!' he said, catching his breath. 'I was so lost in thought that I didn't even hear you come over.'

'How are you feeling?' Thordric asked, indicating the bandages.

'Oh, I'm alright now. The paste Goras gave me has taken the pain away. He thinks the potion you tried to use couldn't handle the Tangle Hold's venom. But I suppose that's not really surprising. We don't have any creatures like that back in Dinia,' he replied, staring at the ground.

'I'm rather glad of that,' Thordric said with a smile, but quickly dropped it as he realised Hamlet was crying. The tears rolled down his face, freezing before they could drop off his chin, forming icicles.

'It was my fault,' Hamlet sniffed, wiping his eyes hastily. 'I could've gotten everyone killed, and it's all because of my stupid curiosity.' His eyes were burning as he spoke, a cold self-loathing in them that Thordric had never seen before.

'That's not true. It could have happened to any of us, stumbling across a dangerous animal like that. If it wasn't for Goras, we would have run into trouble much sooner,' Thordric replied seriously.

'That's not the point,' Hamlet burst out. 'All I do is slow everyone down. When I'm on board *Dinia's Jewel* I can't help with the planning or cooking because I get sick, even with your potions. In Fyoras I collapsed because of those flowers, I couldn't make it up the mountain without your help, and then there was last night...face it, I shouldn't be here, I'm a waste of space.'

Thordric couldn't believe what he was hearing. Hamlet, who he was sure had more knowledge about things than the rest of them put together and who *never* got angry, was shouting, and calling himself a waste of space?

Thordric took a breath. 'So, you get ill a lot and aren't the best at physical activities. What does that matter? Who knows when we'll come across something we need you to research? Or decipher?'

'But I'm only experienced with Dinia's history—'

'Tosh! You can work out anything if you want to, familiar with the history or not. That's what you do all the time. Look the theory you came up with about women having magic hundreds of years ago. No one else from our time would ever have thought of something like that; yet you heard Lyanis and Ourellus tell you it was true. And what's more, even if you couldn't do all that, you're still my friend. I need you here for moral support if nothing else,' he spouted, feeling drained.

Hamlet looked at him, more tears appearing in his eyes. 'Thordric, I—'

'Never mind. All I want you to do is be your usual, excitable self. I can't think properly without you running around enthusiastically and pointing out things even vaguely old and interesting,' he replied, straight faced.

'In that case,' Hamlet said, managing a small lift at the corners of his mouth, 'I suppose I should try to cheer up a little bit.'

It took them three more days to cross the frozen lake, but finally they heard the hooves of their horses hit hard rock below the snow, signalling their return to land.

The Ugamba lived in a forest about a mile away from the edge of the lake and, with great caution, they advanced into it. Goras led the way, his dagger firmly in his hand now, for he warned that there were creatures living in the trees that would jump down and drink their blood if given the slightest chance.

The trees were dense, and the Grosted horses found it hard to manoeuvre around them because of their size. With great reluctance, Goras told the party to dismount and continue on foot. Instantly, they all felt vulnerable and took great care to move as quietly as they could, knowing that if they made the slightest sound, they would end up surrounded by dangerous creatures.

Finally, they made it to the area that Goras knew the Ugamba visited most often, where he'd tried to capture one before. He wanted to make a net out of strips of tree bark, but Lyanis told him not to.

'You won't catch them like that,' she said. 'They're too quick, and their venom, as well as being deadly if they bite you, can also melt any type of net or trap you try and use.'

'How is it you know this?' Goras said, mistrusting her words. They hadn't taken kindly to each other since she'd tried to convince him she was the one who'd taken the Ugamba venom before. He still refused to accept it no matter what she said.

'You'll have to take my word for it,' she answered curtly.

'Then how did you capture one before?' Thordric asked, but it was Ourellus who answered.

'She didn't need to,' he said. 'When mother has her powers, she can encourage any animal to come to her, even if it's not native to her forest. That is one of the great powers of the forest dwellers.'

'Oh,' Thordric said. 'Then how can we do the same now? Her powers are still trapped along with Vey.'

Kal, who had been in conversation with Hamlet about food, spoke up. 'Why don't you capture it with magic? They won't be expecting it, as the people here don't have any.'

Lyanis looked at him. 'That's not a bad idea. All you would need to do is hold it in the air while you extract the venom, then release it back into the trees.'

'That I can do,' Thordric said, 'but how *will* I extract the venom?'

'When people collect snake venom, they make it bite through a cup covered with thin strip of cloth or leather. The venom drips through into the cup; it's quite safe as long as the snake is held securely,' Hamlet said. 'You could try something similar.'

'But the only bottles I have are made of glass,' Thordric said. 'Won't the venom melt that, too?'

'Hmm,' Lyanis mused. 'You may be right. When I collected it, I used a pouch made from a plant resistant to most venoms and poisons. Unfortunately, that particular plant seems to be long extinct.'

'There is plant like that in Numteqa,' Goras grunted. 'Grows near village we came from.'

'Can it handle the strongest of poisons?' Lyanis asked, arching her eyebrow.

'Yes. Even acid does not maim it,' Goras replied, somewhat proudly.

'In that case, I think I have a plan,' she replied. She walked over to Thordric and examined his bag closely. 'If we get one of the Ugamba to bite a piece of this leather,' she said, pointing at one of the straps dangling down from it, 'then it will be coated in venom. It will start to melt it, but I think if you levitate it back with us, then the venom will freeze before it does too much damage. Once we return to the village at the base of the mountain, Goras can show me this plant of his and I'll weave a pouch from it. All we have to do then is melt the venom and let it drip into the pouch.'

'Alright,' said Thordric, wondering if it would really work. 'What do we do now then?'

'We wait. Until nightfall, when they appear,' Goras said, sitting down in the snow as though it wasn't freezing his backside.

As night came, they waited silently for the Ugamba to arrive. Thordric put up another shield around them and, on a whim to see if he could, managed to put one around the Grosted horses back where they'd left them. He knew it was working because

130

he could sense some creatures trying to get inside it at the back of his mind. He was fortunate to find that the Grosted horses didn't move around much, so he could keep the shield around them in a constant place and focus on waiting for the Ugamba instead.

They weren't kept long. As the moon appeared, full and bright in the sky, they heard a scuffling sound in the distance. It grew closer and closer until they saw something scurry out in front of them, pausing to sniff the air. Thordric caught a flash of silver fur and red eyes before it squeaked loudly, picking up their scent.

Suddenly, a hoard of them appeared from the trees, all about as big as his forearm. They advanced as one unit, their teeth bared, ready to attack. But as soon as they got close, they bounced off Thordric's shield. Frustrated, they tried again, but the shield held firm. A great snarl of anger rippled through their ranks. Then they parted; Thordric and the others watched as a single Ugamba came forwards, three times the size of the others, and started clawing away at the shield.

'That's the one you want,' Lyanis whispered to him.

Thordric nodded and, making sure to keep the shields up firmly, he levitated the big one up into the air. It struggled, but realised quickly it was useless, as there was nothing physically holding it that it could bite.

Seizing the opportunity, Thordric stretched out his hands, holding the long leather strap between them so it was taught. He pushed it to the Ugamba's mouth. It took the bait and bit it hard, releasing beads of inky black venom into the leather. Once it was satisfied and had let go, Thordric pulled his arms back inside the shield and released the Ugamba to the ground.

Having just experienced something very strange, it sat up in front of the others and made a terrified chattering sound with its teeth. The others looked at it, sensing its fear, and retreated back into the trees.

'Well, that wasn't so difficult, was it?' Kal said, though Thordric felt like he was about to faint. One of the Ugamba's teeth had been barely an inch from his fingers.

The journey back to the village went without incident, aside from being tailed by a few Snow Spiders, who quickly gave up as the Grosted horses galloped further and further out of their reach.

True to Lyanis's plan, Thordric levitated the venom-coated leather in front of him until it had frozen solid, and once they had dismounted in the village, Goras showed her where the plant she needed was.

With deft fingers, she quickly wove it into a pouch solid enough to keep liquid in. Melting the venom with his magic, Thordric then let it drip into the pouch, making sure he caught every last drop. They held their breath, waiting to see if the plant was truly as impressive as Goras had said. The pouch held fast.

Relieved, they returned to the inn to get some rest before climbing back up the mountain path the next day. However, the moment they walked through the door, Goras boasted about their great success, and made it clear to the innkeeper that they would all spend the night drinking and feasting. Unable to refuse the Numteqians yet again, they woke the following morning feeling worse than they had the first time.

Goras laughed as Thordric stumbled out of his room to pay the innkeeper, who, unlike the merchants of Fyoras, accepted Dinian coins due to the fact that they were made from metals rare to Numteqa. Thordric scowled and tried to swallow down some breakfast.

After they'd recovered enough, and with Thordric saying a last goodbye to the Grosted horses who had carried them safely on their journey, Goras took them back up the mountainside where Grale was awaiting their return.

Not unexpectedly, they found him with several bottles full of different types of alcohol, with more than one of them holding strong whisky. He smiled, bleary eyed, as they came into view. 'Got what you came for, then?' he said, with only a trace of a slur.

Thordric told him what'd happened. Grale whistled. 'Rather you than me,' he said, and once they had prepared themselves and thanked Goras, Grale took them back down the treacherous path to where *Dinia's Jewel* floated silently at the bottom.

They boarded her and headed back to Neathin Valley as they'd promised Grale. As they sailed, having to get used to the speed again after spending over a week on the ground, Thordric set about distilling the Ugamba venom.

It was ready before they reached Valley Edge, and everyone, greatly interested in how the magic would affect him this time, watched as he drank it down in one big gulp. He coughed as he felt it burn his oesophagus, but after a while the burning subsided. He looked down at his hands. What he saw made him dizzy. His nails had turned black and were growing into thick, sharp claws.

'Will this wear off like the effect the herb's magic had did?' he asked Lyanis, terrified.

'No,' she said, making his heart drop. 'But you can reverse the effects yourself once you've mastered its magic and successfully merged it with the other three.'

'The other three?' he said. 'Do you mean I have to stay like this until we've gathered the magic from Wyotis, too?'

'Yes,' she said, looking grim. 'But it shouldn't affect you too badly. After all, it's just your nails. I can clip them down if you like.'

He looked at her nervously, but knew it was a good idea. 'Perhaps you should. They're so sharp I might accidentally cut someone with them.'

They dropped Grale off, helping him unload all the bottles he'd brought back with him, and then Ourellus steered the ship around to head south. Wyotis was the last place they needed to gather magic from. After that, their journey would be complete.

BLACK WAGONS

The morning dawned bleak and cold as they crossed the border into Wyotis. Despite being at the southernmost part of Dinia, it'd only taken them seven hours to get there from where they'd parted with Grale at Neathin Valley.

Thordric had rested for most of the journey along with Hamlet and Kal, but Lyanis stayed up with Ourellus in deep conversation. The magic they needed from Wyotis differed from the others in that it was a human magic, like that of wizard magic in Dinia.

The last time Lyanis had been to Wyotis, there had been five tribes populating the land, each one a thousand strong and terribly ferocious. All five had been led by children born with a strong magic that allowed them to protect their tribe from enemies, for the tribes battled constantly with each other for dominance over the land. Any tribe without a child possessing magic had been wiped out long before.

The books Thordric had found in the library back at the Wizard Council stated that the five tribes still existed and continued to fight each other, but as they'd been written several hundred years ago, before Kalljard sealed Dinia off from the rest of the world, they were hardly reliable.

'We'll have to find a way to bargain with them,' Lyanis was saying as Thordric unrolled himself from his blankets. 'When I came here before, the tribe I approached was the weakest and was about to be attacked by the other four. I used my powers to make the other tribes' horses gallop off in the wrong direction, keeping them safe for a time. In return, they allowed me to take some of the child's magic.'

'But we have no way of knowing what the situation is until we get to where they are. Something like that may not work, even if Thordric uses the other three magics,' Ourellus replied, turning the ship's wheel to avoid a low cloud.

'I'll think of something,' Thordric said, getting up and sorting through their bags for a pot. He filled it with water, and, using his magic, produced a flame beneath it. Once the water was hot, he poured in a bag of oats and stirred them, making porridge.

'How are the magics reacting with each other?' Lyanis asked, scrutinising him thoroughly.

Thordric frowned. 'I don't know; I can't feel them at all.' He looked down at his black nails, which, even though Lyanis had cut them back a few hours ago, were already an inch long again.

'That may be a good sign, though only when you have the fourth will we truly know. Kalljard grew into the magic I placed within him as he grew himself, but you have to adapt to them one by one as a fully grown adult. The process will be very different for you,' she said.

Thordric smiled wryly. If the inspector had heard him being called fully grown, he would have laughed, for Thordric had only grown half an inch in the six years they'd known each other. 'Once we get on the ground, I'll have a go at using them properly; I think I need to rest again before then.'

True to his word, he finished his porridge and fell back to sleep, feeling as though his body was using much more energy than usual. Though he couldn't feel the magics within him anymore, the vividness of his dreams told him that they were still struggling against each other, jousting for dominance.

There was one dream in particular that kept reoccurring. It started with the Criads grazing in their forest, eating a plant that looked very much like the herb from Fyoras. Then, all of a sudden, a swarm of Ugamba attacked them, covering every inch of the Criads' bodies, puncturing their skin to inject the deadly venom. The Criads' antlers, which had been pulsing dully with light, turned an angry red, and luminescent tears fell from the Criads' eyes.

'Thordric, wake up,' Ourellus called, gently shaking his son by the shoulders.

Thordric had been screaming in his sleep, so loudly that everyone had crowded around him to see what was wrong. His eyes flickered open, seeing them all staring down at him. He was panting heavily and sweat dripped from his forehead. It felt like he'd been crying, too.

He glanced down at his hands and inhaled sharply. The black was not only on his fingernails now, but had gone into his veins, making his arms look as though someone had drawn on them with black ink.

'It's too strong for me!' he cried, backing up against the side of the ship. He looked around wildly, afraid that if he did anything, the magic would unleash itself without him being able controlling it.

The dream had gone on longer this time; he'd seen the

Criads reduced to nothing but bone by the Ugamba, and all the plants had been destroyed. He'd known then that the Ugamba magic had absorbed the other two and wanted to break free from him.

'It's alright,' Ourellus said, keeping his tone even. 'You can control it if you want to. You simply have to try.' But Thordric shook his head, muttering over and over again that it was too strong.

'You will be fine, Thordric,' Lyanis said firmly. 'The Criads knew that it was our intention to gather all four magics, not just theirs. If they'd had any doubts about your ability to handle all of them, then they would never have given you their sacred antlers.'

Thordric looked up at her, shaking. 'Then how do I make it stop? How do I control it until we get the last one?' he said, his voice trembling.

'You have to trust in yourself,' she replied, and took over the ship's wheel, which had been left unattended, steering them down to where they could now see vast plains of long grass.

The others, leaving Thordric to calm himself, stood up and peered over the side of the ship. Large black wagons, driven by palomino horses, were moving rapidly across the plains. There were far too many to count, though Hamlet estimated the number was close to two thousand.

'Are they one of the tribes?' he asked Lyanis.

'I would presume so, though I don't remember seeing black wagons before. The tribe I went to had dark blue ones, and the other four were coloured red, purple, brown and gold,' she replied.

'Shall we meet with them?' Ourellus asked, watching the wagons stop. They had obviously spotted the ship, as groups of men were pouring out of them and pointing up towards *Dinia's Jewel*.

However, before Lyanis could reply, they heard several loud whistling sounds and ducked quickly as a wave of arrows hit the ship, some landing on the deck and spearing the wood. One of them had embedded itself where Kal's head had been only moments before. He whimpered as he saw it, scurrying further back.

Thordric stood up, his body moving of its own accord. He climbed onto the side of the ship, balancing there as another wave of arrows hurtled up at them. He waved his hand as they were about to hit him, and they dropped away to the ground.

'Thordric, what are you doing?!' Ourellus shouted, trying to drag him back. Thordric wanted to let him, but his body simply refused to obey and kicked Ourellus back.

Then Thordric was falling.

He could hear the wind rushing at his ears and saw the ground drawing closer, knowing his only chance of survival was to put up a shield to reduce the damage he would receive from the impact. But again, his body refused to listen, and he flipped in the air, landing softly on the ground in a kneeling position, as if he'd only jumped off a small step.

The tribesmen gathered around, nocking fresh arrows to their bows, and aiming them at him. What would he do now? Surely, he couldn't deflect all of them at this close a range?

The magic inside him seemed to think differently. It exploded out like a gale, knocking every man to the ground. He swallowed; he hadn't even felt it building.

Steering the ship down, Ourellus quickly released the ladder so Thordric could climb up. 'Come on, Thordric. This tribe's too aggressive, let's find another—'

He cut off as more tribesmen came towards them, this time making a big show of putting their bows to their sides, signalling that they weren't going to attack. The man in front was holding the hand of a small girl, barely five years old. She was dressed completely in white and had animal fangs decorating her dark hair. Her eyes were a deep purple, cool and collected.

The man let go of her and she walked boldly up to Thordric, who, to his own great relief, had regained some control over his body. She took hold of his hands and stared at them, taking in his black veins and long nails. Then she turned back to the men behind her and made a swift beckoning gesture.

The other tribesmen strode forwards and took hold of Thordric firmly, walking him to their wagons. Before they had gone ten paces, however, Lyanis jumped down the ship's ladder and barked at them in a harsh, snarling language.

The little girl looked at her in surprise and replied back in the same guttural way.

'What are they saying?' Thordric heard Kal whisper to Ourellus as they also climbed down from the ship along with Hamlet.

'How should I know?' he replied. 'This is the first time I've heard it myself!'

Lyanis and the girl continued talking for several more minutes, each getting louder as they spoke. Eventually, Lyanis broke off with a sigh of both relief and expiration.

'They want to take Thordric with them to the battle they're headed to. They were impressed by his powers and want to use them to win,' she explained, as they followed the girl and the tribesmen, still holding Thordric, over to the wagons.

'What shall we do, then?' Hamlet asked.

'We do nothing,' she replied. 'If Thordric helps them win, then the girl has promised to give him some of her own power.'

'You mean I have to fight?' Thordric said, wriggling around in the tribesmen's grips to look at her. 'To...kill people?'

'It looks like it,' she said, a touch of sadness in her voice.

'But I can't do that! I'm a wizard of the council. It's our job to help people, not to cause harm. If they want people killed, then someone else can do it, even if it means leaving without the fourth magic!'

She looked at him but said nothing.

The tribe allowed the others to come with them as long as they could have Thordric and let them sleep in one of the spare wagons. Thordric, meanwhile, had been taken to the head wagon, where the little girl contented herself with giving him food and drink that he continually tried to refuse.

How could such a small girl want him to kill other people so badly? He just couldn't understand it.

He'd tried talking to her, wanting to see if he could reason with her, but she couldn't understand anything he said. After three days, using drawings and sign language to help her understand, he gave up, resenting the whole tribe.

At night, the tribe stopped for their evening meal, giving him the only chance he had of seeing the others. Each of them looked tired and worn, having been made to walk on foot during the day.

'How have they been treating you?' Thordric asked as they sat down next to him in front of the fire. He couldn't help thinking that if he'd have gained control over the magic within him, they could have found a different tribe and helped them in a more peaceful way, like Lyanis had before.

'Well, we haven't rested our feet properly since we arrived,' Kal said, tucking into the bowl of hot vegetable stew that had been given to him by the tribeswoman serving. 'But Lyanis has been able to find out more about them.'

'Really?' Thordric asked.

'They didn't mind me talking to them, so I managed to ask lots of questions,' she said, taking a mouthful of stew. 'There are only two tribes left now, and this one is made up of the tribes that had red, purple and blue wagons that I saw so long ago. They all fell to the gold tribe and the survivors grouped together for the sole purpose of getting their revenge. That was three hundred years ago, but only now have they built up their numbers enough to try. They've been avoiding the gold tribe for years, letting them farm the land as much as they want. As a result, the gold tribe no longer roam around, but live in a city built with strong walls.'

'So, this tribe wants to start a siege?' Thordric said, thinking that if they only had to capture the city, he could get away without hurting anyone.

'Unfortunately, not,' she replied, reading his mind. 'They felt that a siege would not fully satisfy their revenge, and so sent messengers to the city to inform them of their advance. It seems the gold tribe accepted their challenge, for the messengers have not returned.'

Thordric banged his fist on the floor. 'This is ridiculous!' he said. 'Why are we getting caught up in a war when all we're trying to do is save Vey?'

'We knew this quest would be difficult before we started out,' Ourellus said quietly. 'I know you don't want to go along with it, but if we attempt to escape, they may very well try to kill us.'

They all stared silently into the flames, the light reflecting in their eyes.

'Maybe you *don't* have to kill anyone,' Hamlet said slowly, eyeing Thordric.

'What do you mean?' Thordric asked, wondering what his friend was thinking.

'Well, the magic inside you is strong, isn't it? What if you use it to *pretend* to attack the gold tribe, but instead cause damage to both? You don't have to hurt anyone, merely break up their wagons and the city walls or something,' he explained.

'But how does that help?' Thordric asked, confused. 'The tribes want to kill each other; I don't see how damaging their property affects that.'

'If you do it well enough and put on a big show of exactly how powerful you are, they might start to revere you and come together as one because of it,' Hamlet said.

'Or they'll both turn on him and want him dead instead,' Kal said gloomily.

'Maybe so, but even then Thordric's got enough power to stop them. Haven't you, Thordric?' Hamlet said, looking at him confidently.

'That may be true,' Thordric admitted. 'But I still can't control it. What if I accidentally wipe everyone out?'

Ourellus put his hand on his shoulder. 'You won't. We all have faith in you, though I think this plan needs a little tweaking before we try it.'

17

CITY OF GOLD

The horses pulling the wagon stopped abruptly, making it jolt. Thordric, who had been feigning sleep to try and stop the little girl from feeding him, was thrown forwards by a few feet. He sat up, listening to the excited chatter coming from outside. Before he could wonder what was going on, a head popped through the flap of the wagon. It was one of the tribesmen who had been at the very head of the party.

He spoke briefly to the girl and threw a glance at Thordric, before leaving as more excited voices could be heard. The girl turned to Thordric, a wide smile on her face.

'We have reached the gold tribe's city,' she said in Dinian, though her accent was still harsh and guttural.

'You can speak my language?' he asked, surprised. Then the full implications of such a realisation sank in. He and the others had managed snatched conversations about their plans every time they met, yet the last two times, when they were going over the finalities of it, the girl had been sitting right next to him.

'Yes,' she said, her eyes glittering. 'The magic I possess

allows me to learn languages simply by hearing them a few times. It took me some days, but now I have mastered it.' She stood up, brushing her white gown free of the coloured powders she'd been using to paint with. 'You should know that the plan you have will not work. I will not allow it.'

'And how do you intend to stop me?' he snapped, irritated by the sheer delight she took from the idea. 'I have three great magics within me, as well as my own. They're much stronger than yours.'

'Your magics may be stronger in power, but there is no way you can override mine,' she said. Her eyes bore into him as she spoke, smiling even more wickedly.

'Rubbish, I can—'

He was cut off as pain cracked through his spine, as though he'd been struck by lightning. He collapsed over to the side, unable to move.

'Do you understand, now?' the girl said, and as she bent down to examine his face, Thordric got a good look at her eyes. They were wide and crazed, and something flitted within them that caused a tremor of pure horror to shoot through him.

This was no little girl he was dealing with. She was possessed by a monster, and it was manipulating not only her, but the whole tribe as well. If the child from the gold tribe was also possessed in this way, then it wasn't the people that really wanted war, it was the monsters.

Two tribesmen came into the wagon and picked Thordric up at the girl's command, dragging him outside to a grassy knoll, where more people slowly trickled to as they made their way over from their wagons.

As the sun broke through a large stretch of cloud in the sky, Thordric laid eyes on the city of the gold tribe.

It was a fortress of high, jagged walls decorated with gold leaf. At the top were large spikes, preventing any attackers from scaling up them to sneak inside. It looked even larger than the royal city in Fyoras.

As the sunlight reflected off it, Thordric couldn't decide whether it was beautiful or horrifying, and as he listened, he could clearly hear movement going on behind its golden gates.

A loud boom swept across the entire plain as a cannonball flew straight to where Thordric was standing. Before he had time to think about it, he put up a strong shield and the cannon-ball bounced off to land heavily on the ground.

It was the first time he'd used magic since the tribe had taken him, but whether it was his own magic he'd drawn upon or the other three magics inside him, he wasn't sure. What he *was* sure about, however, was that this time he'd been the one in control.

Another cannonball shot through the air, and then another and another. Thordric blocked them all, every one of them dropping at his feet. There was silence, and then the golden gates of the city opened.

Along with the heavy grinding of their hinges, a great roar erupted from inside, uttered by tribesmen dressed in gold-painted leathers. They carried golden swords, spears, and bows, and as soon as the gates were open fully, they rushed out in one big mass, spilling onto the plain to face the black tribe's army.

Then it began.

Both sides flew at each other, swinging their swords franti-cally and without any form of military tactics at all. Archers from both tribes rained down scores of arrows, sometimes hitting enemy, sometimes hitting friend. Thordric, caught in the middle of it all, cowered down to the ground, putting up a shield so that he didn't get trodden on – or worse.

He had no idea where the others were, hoping they were far away from the fighting, safe in one of the back wagons almost a mile from where he was.

He crawled around, trying to find a way back to them through the great sea of legs surrounding him. His shield made several people fall to the side, but he was in too much of a rush to worry about whether he had caused anyone to be wounded because of it. When at last he was out of the main mass of people, he stood up, startling a few stragglers who were hurrying to join in. He ran past them to the relative safety of the wagons, but when he got there, he found the little girl standing in wait for him.

'You were supposed to fight!' she spat, her fury firing out in her voice. 'My tribe is dying because you refuse to help!'

'Your tribe is dying because you goaded them into a meaningless battle,' he breathed, his own anger welling up inside him. 'Tell me, how long have you possessed that girl?'

'Oh, so you noticed, did you?' she said, hissing slightly. 'Very few do, and I usually have them killed if they become a nuisance. You won't become a nuisance, will you?'

She turned her head to look at something behind her. Thordric followed her gaze and gasped in horror. Ourellus, Kal, Lyanis and Hamlet were chained together so tightly that their skin was raw. They were staring back at her with a mix of terror and contempt. 'Fight for me, and your friends will go unharmed. Refuse, and things may not end well for them.'

Smiling wickedly, she flicked her hand in their direction. Instantly, they all let out shrieks of pain, writhing around as though they were being electrocuted. As he'd personally experienced it, this time Thordric felt the magic pulsating out of her, and he could tell it was only half of what she was capable of.

Despite being in agony, Ourellus called out to Thordric. 'There is...always...another way,' he gasped, sweat trickling down his brow.

'Silence!' the girl screamed at him, intensifying her magic

so much that he foamed at the mouth. She turned back to Thordric, the shadow in her eyes more evident than ever. 'You *will* fight, or they *will* die,' she said.

Yet Thordric knew his father was right. There was always another way; he just had to think what it was. A way not only to stop the fighting, but to chase the monsters out of the little girl and her counterpart in the golden tribe.

The magic inside him suddenly jumped into life and lashed out at the girl, knocking her back against one of the wagons. She hit it with a sickening crack and fell hard to the ground.

Thordric fought to take control of the magic again, but it was filling him up, feeding on his fright and anger like some kind of leech. Gritting his teeth and using every part of his being, he shoved it back down. It was working, but something hard hit his head and he fell to the floor. The magic within seized its chance and exploded out once again, but this time it flattened the entire area.

Wagons, horses, people – everything was forced to the ground. The wave even reached the gold tribe's city, making the walls buckle and fall in upon themselves. Large chunks of it smashed down around everyone, bringing instant death to those who were unfortunate enough to be in the way.

It was the last thing Thordric saw before he slipped into darkness.

Someone was rubbing a cold liquid onto his head.

His eyes opened slowly, and he saw Lyanis, her face badly cut, looking down at him. She inhaled sharply as she saw he was awake, her mouth breaking into a smile of relief.

'Ourellus!' she called. 'He's awake.'

Ourellus's face appeared above him, too. He looked pale,

and his lips were chapped and raw. 'Thank goodness he's alright,' he murmured, and Thordric noticed a tear running down his face.

'What happened?' Thordric asked, trying to sit up. His whole body felt weak and shook with the effort. Lyanis and Ourellus put their hands on his shoulders, supporting him until he was in a comfortable position.

'You knocked everybody out,' Ourellus said. 'Including us, but the blast's main wave travelled towards the city, so it didn't affect us as much. It did break those chains, though.'

'What about Hamlet and Kal?' he asked, realising that they weren't there. 'Where are they?'

'They're alright,' Lyanis replied. 'One of the wagons fell on top of them. We managed to pull it off, but they're both quite injured.'

Thordric swallowed. 'They...they are?'

'It's nothing life threatening. Hamlet's got a broken leg and Kal's shoulder was dislocated, and they both received a few large splinters. I've bandaged them as much as I could, and I used some of that orange potion you had in your pocket to lessen some of their bruises, but we needed to find someone who could help them properly. That's why we're here,' she said.

He looked around him. They were in a small room decorated with gold furnishings, with a sink and a large water jug in one corner and a bath in the other. He found that he was lying on a bed of soft rushes on the floor, covered in blankets woven with gold thread.

'Are we where I think we are?' he asked them.

'We're in what's left of the gold tribe's city,' Ourellus replied. 'Most of the people fled after they saw both the armies flattened, but a few remained, including one of the healers here. He's attending to Hamlet and Kal now.'

'A healer? You mean like a doctor?' he asked.

'Doctor? Oh, yes, that's what you call healers in Dinia now, isn't it?' Lyanis mused. She turned to Ourellus. 'I believe you mentioned Thordric's mother was training to be one when you first met her.'

Ourellus blushed. 'Yes, she was,' he replied, coughing uncomfortably. 'Anyway, we told the healer that we were prisoners of the black tribe, and after everything that's happened, he decided to help us. We brought the girl, too. She's still unconscious, though, and she's suffered a lot of bruising to her spine.'

Thordric looked around the room again and saw what he had first thought was a pile of rags, but in fact was the little girl, tied up and covered in blankets. 'Did you realise it too?' he asked, looking from her to them.

'Realise what?' Ourellus asked, raising his eyebrow.

'The girl. She's possessed by something. I think the child here might be as well.'

'Possessed?' Lyanis asked in surprise, but then her eyes narrowed. 'Did you see a flicker in her eyes?'

'I didn't just see it, I felt it. When she was angry. I think it's been controlling the whole tribe through her.'

'The girl I took the magic from last time also had a strange flicker in her eyes. She was the same age as this one, but she acted far older than her years. When I managed to redirect the other tribes, I caught a glimpse of the children leading them, too. If I remember rightly, they were also the same age.'

'Do you think they're the same ones, then? The surviving two?' Ourellus asked her sharply.

'No, I don't think it's that...' Lyanis said. 'More like whatever is possessing them stays within the children until they reach a certain age. Then it moves on to another host.'

'If that's true, then what happens to the children these

monsters leave?' Thordric asked, looking at the girl again, who was beginning to stir.

'I don't know. This is all speculation, anyway.' She smiled at him, and he got the feeling an idea was forming in her mind. 'I know a way you could find out though, as I doubt she'll be willing to tell us.'

'Don't push him, mother,' Ourellus said, apparently arriving at the same idea. 'Let him recover first.'

'What is it?' Thordric asked them, turning from one to the other.

'Do you remember us saying that the magic of the Ugamba allows you to control creatures?' Lyanis said. Thordric did. 'Well, whatever is possessing her is probably something you can do that to. It shouldn't affect her real self, as it only works on conscious minds, and I suspect hers has been buried deep inside for years while the creature holds command.'

'I can't use that magic at will, though. I believed I could at one point, but what happened at the battle proves that it still acts on its own,' Thordric said, hearing his voice quiver at the thought of the sheer power of the Ugamba's magic. The very thought of using it when it could cause so much destruction made him feel ill.

'I have a theory about that, actually,' Ourellus said. 'When you lost control over it on the ship, you ended up protecting us with it, the same as when the tribesmen surrounded you and you knocked them over. What happened at the battle was actually very similar; it was only when you saw us getting hurt that it rushed out of you. It's not appearing at random, it's doing it when you want to protect people. That doesn't mean that you have complete control over it, but unconsciously, you *are* using it how you want to.'

He checked the little girl, making sure that she wasn't fully awake yet. 'Don't you remember our plan? It was to fake going into battle, and instead destroy enough of the city and the wagons to make them afraid of you so they'd then listen to what you had to say. When the magic released itself during the battle, that's almost exactly what happened,' he continued, unable to stop himself from grinning at his son.

Thordric thought about it, realising his father was right. 'So, you really think I can control it if I want to?' he asked.

'Yes, I do,' Ourellus replied. 'And by the looks of it, the opportunity to try is right now.' He indicated the girl, who was now sitting upright, struggling with the tight rope they'd tied her with.

'It's no use,' Ourellus told her. 'I strengthened that rope with magic, and yours isn't of the same type to be able to break it.'

Thordric looked at him. 'You can use your magic properly again?' he said.

'It seems that way,' Ourellus replied. 'I had to try it, otherwise she'd have escaped already.'

'But she's been unconscious since the battle,' Thordric said, puzzled.

'Actually, she woke up not long after we did. I had to knock her out again,' he explained.

'How did you do that?' Thordric asked, unable to imagine him hitting her.

Ourellus smirked. 'Did you happen to count the bottles that Grale had with him?'

Thordric hadn't.

'There was one less when he got off the ship,' Ourellus said. 'It was strong whisky. I gave her a large cup of it.'

18

SHADOW SEEKER

'So that's what you forced down me, is it?' the little girl hissed. 'You chose to poison this poor young child's body with alcohol to knock me out, did you?'

The flicker in her eyes was more evident now; the creature possessing her had obviously given up trying to hide.

'It won't hurt her,' Ourellus said, unaffected by the creature's attempt to make him feel guilty. 'You might feel that she has an ache to her head, but that will wear off. Now, why don't you tell us exactly what you are?'

'And why would I do that? You have no way of making me talk,' she said, staring them down defiantly.

'Actually, we do,' Lyanis replied, smiling at her sweetly.

'It's not nice for a lady to lie, particularly when she's as ugly as you,' the girl said, batting her eyelids.

The smile on Lyanis's face vanished. 'You're lucky you *are* possessing such a young child,' she said. 'Or I might have struck you for that.' She turned, meeting Thordric's gaze. He got up and went over to the girl, sitting a few paces in front of her.

'*You!*' the girl said, realising who he was. He felt her magic rise and knew that she was planning to attack him again. Trying to remain calm, he raised a shield around himself, one purely for use against magical attacks. To do it, he used both his own magic and the other three that were inside him, noticing that it was getting easier to use them together. Ourellus had told him that once he had the last form of magic, they would merge so well that he wouldn't know what form of magic he was using for his spells.

The girl shrank back as her magic bounced off his shield. Her eyes flickered intensely and grew wide. 'What did you do?' she cried. 'How are you able to withstand my powers?'

'I didn't,' he said calmly. 'I blocked it. Now, are you sure you won't talk to us before we use force?'

She glared at him, as though he had deeply insulted her.

'Fine, then,' he sighed. Concentrating, he pictured her telling them everything she knew about the tribes, what was really possessing her and why she wanted a war so much. Then he willed it to happen.

He felt the magic slowly seeping out of him and into the girl's mind. She struggled, trying to resist it, but he let it pour out a bit more until finally he felt her guard drop and she was fully under his control.

He gestured to Ourellus, who stepped forwards to question her. 'Let's try again,' Ourellus began. 'What is your name, creature, and why have you possessed this young girl?'

This time the girl answered immediately, at Thordric's will. 'My name is Sulvarda. I am a Shadow Seeker. Once we were a species that ruled this land, but that was before the humans came. We tried to possess them to make them leave, but there were too few of us. They condemned the people we'd taken control of as insane and murdered them. There were also times when the vessel we had chosen could only harbour us for a few days before it rotted and died.

'As the humans grew stronger, we grew weaker, having our food and resources taken from us. We were about to give up hope and try to find a home somewhere else, but then a child was born with a great magic inside her. It drew us to her, as we had not seen magic in our lands before. We watched her closely while living on the human's wasted food as best as we could. She grew up and married, bearing many children with magic also. Curious, we decided to possess one and found that these children with magic could withstand us in their bodies for up to five years, longer if we were careful with them. But we could not possess them continually like that, for we wanted them to grow and produce heirs that would also have magic, creating a long family line that one day we could take control of and use them to make the humans leave our homeland.

'Unfortunately, a few hundred years later, the humans had disagreements with each other and split into different tribes, each with several children born with magic. However, we used this to our advantage, using the children's magic to make the tribes revere them and turn against each other. It was our plan to have the tribes wipe each other out, but the battles lasted much longer than any of us could know. They raged for so many years that both we and the humans began to forget the original reason for such turmoil. Then one tribe was finally slain. We thought we would rejoice, but then it was revealed that our brother Shadow Seeker had been destroyed along with his host. My brothers and I grew angry, not knowing who had caused this to happen, and our hatred for our own kind grew as much as that for the humans.

'Eventually, there were five tribes remaining from the original one hundred, and for a while it stayed that way. We had occasional skirmishes with each other, but three hundred years ago the gold tribe came at the others with force and nearly destroyed them all. Yet I survived and managed to convince the human survivors to band together to form the black tribe and rally against the gold tribe, building up our strength and numbers until we could go at them full force. Hence my delight when Thordric turned up, revealing such powerful magic. It was what we needed to beat them...but due to my confidence in the promise the forest dweller made, my plan failed.'

'So, it is true that you jump from child to child when their body starts to fail you?' Lyanis said, without showing a trace of sympathy for the creature.

'Yes,' the girl said unemotionally. 'This one is almost out of time, yet the replacement for her has not been born yet. The mother is back at the camp where we left the other pregnant women.'

Lyanis looked as though she really was going to strike her, but Thordric interrupted. 'Is there a child from the gold tribe possessed like her?' he said.

'There is. Your magic may have flattened the gold tribe's army, but my brother will probably have fled out of harm's way by now. I cannot tell, nor do I care. I have used up the last of my energy and wish to die in peace.'

She closed her eyes then, sinking back to the floor. Thordric watched her, but then his magic left her mind sharply. He rushed over to her, shaking her small body, trying to see if either her or the Shadow Seeker were still alive, but she was no longer breathing. He put his hand on her throat, checking to see if she had a pulse, but as he did so, he saw that the skin underneath the collar of her dress was black and rotten.

Unbidden, tears rolled down his face as he turned to Lyanis and Ourellus to tell them she was dead, the Shadow Seeker along with her.

Ourellus swore, muttering curses that Thordric had never even heard of, and Lyanis sank to her knees in the corner. 'The poor child. Her mind would have been trapped by that creature for her whole life, and now she's gone never having known what it was like to live freely,' she sobbed. Then she looked up at them both with a fire in her eyes. 'We must find the other one. Perhaps it's not too late to save the child it's possessing.'

'Perhaps. And that would also give Thordric the opportunity to gather the magic he needs,' he said. But Thordric wasn't paying attention.

A soft wave-like sensation was flowing through his hands where he was still holding the little girl's body. It crept up his arms into his chest, and then radiated from his core to the rest of his body. It felt similar to when he'd gathered the other magics, but it was kinder, somehow. It was like the hugs his mother used to give him when he was upset as a child, comforting, and making everything else fade into the background.

It reached the other magics inside him and wrapped them in the same comforting hold, and then...all the sensations were gone. The only magic he could feel inside him now was his own, exactly the same as before, when he'd been back at the Wizard Council. Only now he knew it was much more powerful.

Staring at his black fingernails and veins, he willed them to turn back to normal. Effortlessly, they did.

'I have it,' he said softly to Lyanis and Ourellus. 'The fourth magic. It flowed into me from the girl's body.'

They both looked at him, amazed. 'But I don't understand, it couldn't have passed into you when she was already dead,' Lyanis said, wiping a few remaining tears from her smooth face.

'I don't know if I'm right,' Thordric said slowly, 'but I think the little girl knew what was happening and wanted to give it to me. That's the only thing I can think of.'

'We should bury her, and the rest of the people who fell in the battle,' Ourellus said. 'I'll ask the healer if he can take care of the wounded from both sides. Now that one Shadow Seeker is dead and the other is in hiding, there's no more reason for the people to fight.'

It was a sad task, burying the bodies of all the tribesmen and women who had died in the battle. Most of those who had been fighting when Thordric released his magic had merely been knocked unconscious, but a few of them had been killed by the falling rubble. Full of remorse, he dug their graves by hand, not even attempting to use magic.

Some of the survivors from both the black and the gold tribe helped dig the remaining graves, but even with so many people working, it still took three days to finish. As the last grave was filled on the third day, Thordric sat down, exhausted, and rested his shovel against a nearby tree.

Ever since he'd received the fourth magic, flashes of something kept popping into his mind, flitting from image to image, showing him many different places in quick succession. Only now, when at last he'd sat down to relax, did he finally understand what it was.

It was the side power of the herb magic from Fyoras – foresight, Lyanis had called it – showing him images of the future. He saw one very clearly, detailing a small boy running barefoot across the plains, dirty and wearing clothing that had once been smart, but was now tattered and torn.

'Ourellus,' he called, as his father came into sight carrying a flask of water for them both.

'What is it?' Ourellus asked urgently, coming to sit beside him. 'Nothing's happened, has it?'

'Not exactly. It's just that I've seen the child controlled by the other Shadow Seeker.'

'What?' Ourellus said, sitting up and casting his eyes about him. 'Where?'

'In my head. The...foresight, or whatever it is that the royal family in Fyoras can use...I've got it too.'

'Really?' Ourellus asked, a broad grin spreading across his face. 'Then can you tell where the shadow seeker is?'

Thordric shook his head. 'All I've seen is glimpses. It's a boy we're looking for, dressed in smart clothing that's all grubby. I saw him running across a wide plain, but there's so many here that I couldn't tell where it was.'

Ourellus frowned. 'Hmm. At least we know who we're looking for, and that he's not lurking in the city grounds anywhere. How old do you think he was?'

'About five, the same as the little girl.'

'Well, he won't get very far on foot,' Ourellus said, sitting back. 'What did you want to do about the city?'

'You mean, do I want to rebuild it?' Thordric asked. It was something he had been thinking about for a while now. The tribes seemed to be mixing together without much hostility, now that there were no Shadow Seekers trying to control them, and Thordric felt incredibly guilty about destroying their home and the wagons the black tribe had ridden there with, though he knew most of the horses pulling them had survived. 'I know we should really hurry back to Vey as quickly as we can, but it wouldn't feel right if I left it the way it is.'

'I thought you'd say that,' Ourellus said, putting a hand on his shoulder proudly. 'It'll give Kal and Hamlet a bit longer to recover too.'

Thordric grinned back at him. Even though they looked almost the same age, Thordric couldn't help feeling closer to his father the more time they spent together.

They got up and went inside the ruins of the city to the dining hall, where the women had been serving hot food for everyone who'd been helping dig the graves. Lyanis was among them, cutting up ingredients for the stew they were currently making.

As they sat down at a table near the kitchens, they could see one of the other women talking to her animatedly, making her lose concentration and cut the potato she was holding into several jagged lumps instead of neat ones. She looked up and saw them watching her, so she put down her knife and headed over.

'Dinner will be ready soon,' she said, handing them a hot drink that was popular in the city and tasted vaguely of peppermint.

'I've never seen you looking so domestic, mother,' Ourellus said, smirking.

She shot him a dirty look, flicking him with a dishcloth she'd been resting on her shoulder, but then smiled. 'I wouldn't mind it, but one of the women keeps on calling me "child" and asking if I'm betrothed to anyone.'

Ourellus and Thordric snorted. None of the women in the city, or even the world, now that they thought about it, were even close to a tenth of her age. Unfortunately, they made the mistake of reminding her of that fact, to which she responded by returning to the kitchen and coming back with a bucket full of ice water. Taking careful aim, she tipped it right over their heads.

They left rather quickly after, only daring to return at nightfall to steal a loaf of bread.

19

TRAPPED

Thordric and Ourellus surveyed the city's outer walls to see how extensive the damage was. The entire north facing wall was destroyed, being the one that had faced the battle and so received the full brunt of Thordric's magic, and the east and west walls were both cracked down the middle. The south wall, however, remained standing with barely any marks on it at all.

'Do you need any help?' Ourellus asked as he watched his son roll up his sleeves in preparation to begin rebuilding.

'I don't think so, I've fixed buildings quite a few times before, and even though this is bigger than any of those, my magic is much stronger now,' Thordric replied confidently.

'All right, then. I'll go and help Kal fix some of the inner buildings. His shoulder is fine now, so he should be okay to work if he goes easy,' Ourellus said, turning to go back into the city.

'Be careful, he can get quite carried away. And if anything starts smoking, you'll have to stop him quickly before it blows up,' Thordric warned. Ourellus pulled a sceptical expression. 'Trust me,' Thordric added. 'I've had experience of that before. He nearly singed my eyebrows off.'

Ourellus managed a nod and quickly walked off to find Kal, hoping that Thordric was exaggerating.

Turning back to the north facing wall, Thordric stared at the rubble at his feet, deciding how to repair it. When he'd fixed houses before, he usually levitated all the bricks back into place and made the mortar between them wet again, then waited for it to dry. But there were no bricks to put together this time. The wall had been carved out of a single piece of rock. He'd thought about trying to find a new piece and carving them afresh, but the merchants inside the city had already told him that there weren't any deposits of that type of rock left in Wyotis, not to mention they'd long since run out of the gold leaf that covered them.

The only thing he could do was merge the rock back into one piece again and hope it ended up in the right shape. Using the full extent of his new magic, he levitated every piece of rubble from the north wall, including the great piles of dust that had blown across the grass, and spread it all out so that nothing overlapped, becoming the same shape as the wall had been originally. Then he thought of it all returning to a single piece, drawn back together like iron filings to a magnet.

It took a lot of concentration to keep the image of the solid wall in his mind, but he kept on pouring his magic into the rock fragments, urging them to merge like he was visualising in his head. Then, with a sound between a rumble and a grind, the rock finally fused. Thordric looked up to admire his work, but as soon as his eyes reached the centre line, his face fell.

Somehow, he'd managed to make it bulge out like a large wart. He tried separating the particles of that particular piece, but he used too much force and the whole wall came crumbling down again.

He sat down in the cloud of dust that had spread up around him, depressed and in need of a break. He felt something bulging in his pocket, digging into his thigh. Curious, he pulled it out. It was the long-distance communicator, though the small blue flower that poked out of the top (which was in fact the active part that made it work) looked decidedly crumpled. Unscrewing the box, Thordric poured some water from his flask into the flower's container beside the mechanism, adding some magic in with it so that the flower would spring up quicker than normal. He screwed the box back up and waited.

Within moments, the flower perked up and sat bobbing happily out of the hole in the top. With a sudden pang of homesickness, he decided to call Lizzie and see how she was doing back at the council, hoping that his mother and sisters and the inspector were alright as well.

He pressed the single button on the communicator's box. 'Lizzie?' he said, speaking into it.

There was no answer, so he tried again. 'Lizzie, are you there?'

'Thordric, is that you?' came a muffled reply, sounding as though someone had picked up the communicator not knowing how to use it properly.

Thordric blinked. It hadn't been Lizzie who'd spoken, but his friend, Wizard Batsu. 'Batsu? Where's Lizzie? Is something the matter?' he asked, his immediate concern leaking out in his voice.

Batsu laughed. 'No, nothing's wrong. Lizzie's just, er, busy at the moment,' he said.

Thordric's eyes narrowed. It was very unlike Lizzie not to have the communicator with her. The only time she left it somewhere else was at night when she went to bed, but it was the middle of the day.

'Are you sure?' Thordric asked suspiciously.

'Of course. She went down to the Training Facility to make sure that the students were all being taught correctly and were not falling behind because they misunderstood something,' Batsu told him, yet there was something in his voice that told Thordric he wasn't telling the whole truth.

If Batsu was lying to him, then it meant either one of two things. Either Lizzie was up to something that she didn't want him to know about, or something serious had happened to her and he was trying to smooth it over so Thordric wouldn't panic and come rushing back without freeing Vey. He hoped it wasn't the latter.

'Batsu, please tell me what's going on,' he pleaded, as a long train of scenarios of Lizzie getting hurt chugged through his head.

Batsu coughed. 'Well, alright, but don't tell her that I told you. We had some more trouble with Wizard Ayek. He enticed Wizard Rarn to put *Euphoric Dancing Powder* in all the robes of those at the Training Facility. It had them running out into town disrupting everyone going about their business, dancing wildly on the roof of the Young Scholar's Academy and the stationhouse, right when Lizzie was in an important meeting with the Potion Trading Company.'

'What?' Thordric spluttered. 'What did she do?'

'Nothing. She continued with the meeting as if she'd had no interruptions at all.'

'And afterwards? When the meeting was over?' Thordric pressed.

'Oh, that was when she called the inspector and asked for Wizard Ayek and Wizard Rarn to be clapped in chains and suspended from the dining hall ceiling until they were sorry for what they'd done. She's having them let down now, I think. Of course, she asked all of us to help cure the students of their euphoric dancing, so everything is back to normal again.'

Thordric gulped. 'I see.'

'So,' Batsu continued cheerfully, 'how is your journey going? Have you gathered all the magics yet?'

'Uh, yes, actually. But we've had a few hiccoughs along the way,' he admitted.

He explained what'd happened since they'd arrived in Wyotis, right up to trying to fix the walls and waiting for his foresight to kick in again so they could try and track the boy possessed by the remaining Shadow Seeker. Batsu was impressed at what Thordric was now capable of but horrified to hear about the battle.

'I suppose I'd better get back to repairing these walls,' Thordric said after an hour had passed. 'Will you tell Lizzie that we should be home soon?'

'I will,' Batsu replied, and then his voice was gone.

Thordric put the communicator away again, looking at the rubble that was once again strewn at his feet. 'Spells!' he cursed. 'I wish this wall would mend itself!'

As though it had been waiting for that very command, it did. Thordric stared at it, his mouth hanging open. He knew it had been his magic acting on his subconscious again but seeing rubble spring up off the floor and turn into a perfectly solid wall without him even trying was something he didn't see every day.

He was about to go and check if it would work on the other two sides when another image flashed into his mind. He stopped and swore again. This time the image was very clear; the boy they were after had been running across the plains again, but in the distance, he'd seen *Dinia's Jewel*. The boy was heading straight for it.

Without thinking, he shouted at the east and west walls to

fix themselves, which they obediently did, before running back inside the city to get the others.

'What is it, Thordric?' Lyanis asked as he almost ran into her, panting heavily. She had been up in the healer's rooms, visiting Hamlet.

'The boy. I know where he is, or where he will be; I'm not sure,' he breathed, so quickly that she had to make him repeat himself. 'The boy possessed by the Shadow Seeker – he's heading towards *Dinia's Jewel*,' he explained further.

'The ship? But you don't suppose he plans to sail it, do you?' she asked, as they sped down to where Ourellus and Kal were fixing the buildings. It wasn't hard to locate them; there had been several loud bangs that Thordric had identified as Kal's magic getting out of hand.

'That's what it looked like to me. We left the ladder down, so all he has to do is climb up.'

They reached the other two, catching Ourellus scolding Kal for not concentrating hard enough, and Kal spitting back that he was worse to work with than Thordric. Too panicked to even take offence, Thordric cut across them and revealed what he'd seen.

'But what can we do to stop him?' Kal said, his back firmly to Ourellus. 'If he's already nearly there, then we won't be able to catch him before he boards her.'

'He's right,' Ourellus said, though he, too, was facing away. 'We've only got the wagons, and that would take us far too long. By the time we reached the area, he'd already be gone.'

'It's a shame we couldn't have caught him while he was still around here. If we'd have known he was going to escape, we could have left a trap for him—' Kal began, but he stopped at the look on Thordric's face. 'What is it?'

'You've given me an idea, though I don't know if it'll work,' he said, his eyes lighting up as his mind churned out ideas. 'I might be able to put a shield around the ship.'

'That would stop him from getting on,' Lyanis agreed. 'But even if it does work from this distance, it won't stop the boy from getting away on foot again.'

Thordric sighed. 'You're right,' he said, but this time it was Ourellus who had an idea.

'Do you think you could reverse a shield?' he asked. 'So that instead of keeping him out, it would keep him in?'

Thordric stared at his father. It was a brilliant idea. 'I can try,' he said. 'Though I'll have to practice first.'

'That may be wise, but you can't take too long over it. If he's really as close to the ship as you say he is, we don't have very long,' Lyanis said.

'I know,' Thordric said. 'Kal can help me get it right.'

'I...I can?' Kal said.

'Yes. I'm going to try putting a reverse shield around you, and I want to see if you can get out of it.'

'Okay,' Kal said, somewhat apprehensively. He readied himself as Thordric thought about the process needed to make it work.

Using his magic to push in at Kal instead of out, Thordric concentrated on keeping the pressure he was using even, making sure that there were no weak points. It was hard, after training himself for so long to focus on reflecting objects to suddenly switch to containing them, but once he got his mind over that, he managed to do it easily.

Kal tried to move forwards, walking two paces before hitting the shield. He did the same at each point; it was holding.

'You haven't thought about doing this to him before, have you?' Ourellus joked in Thordric's ear. Kal heard him and scowled as Thordric's head fell to his chest as another image flashed into his mind.

The boy was there, climbing up onto the ship's deck already. Given that they'd worked out his foresight was only showing him things a few minutes ahead of time, judging by how high the sun had been in each vision, he knew that he had to get ready to put the reverse shield over the boy now, or else he would lose his chance.

Thordric pictured the area surrounding the ship clearly in his mind, the images helping him where his memory was hazy. Not knowing exactly where the boy was at that moment, he cast a large reverse shield all the way around it, hoping to trap him in it even if he hadn't gotten on the ship yet.

'Did it work?' Kal asked beside him as Thordric brought his mind back to where he was standing.

'I think so,' Thordric said, hoping that he'd made the reverse shield strong enough all over. 'The only way we can know for sure, though, is if I have another vision.'

Unsure what to do, they all waited breathlessly in the hope a vision would appear. The urge to rush off and check was strong, but they all knew it would be pointless. If the boy was trapped, then he'd still be trapped by the time they got there. If not, then even travelling at their fastest, they could never catch up to the speed of *Dinia's Jewel*.

Trying to take their minds off it, they all helped to repair the buildings in the inner city. Thordric was anxious about using his magic for other things when he wasn't sure if his shield had worked properly, but he could feel it there still, holding up in the back of his mind.

When he saw Kal and Ourellus trying to work together, however, he had to use his magic simply to fix all the damage they'd caused disagreeing with each other on how to repair things. Slowly, the buildings took shape back to how they'd been, with Thordric ending up doing most of it himself. He was just fixing the last window in city when his foresight flashed an image into his mind.

It was the one they'd been waiting for, and as Thordric called the others to tell them, he smiled. His shield really had worked, and the boy was trapped on *Dinia's Jewel*, now eating most of the food.

They all sighed with relief upon hearing the news and went up to the healer's rooms to tell Hamlet.

The cast on his leg was being changed when they arrived, meaning they had to wait before they could see him. When the healer had finished, they rushed over and explained what had happened, though they were amused to find that Hamlet was more horrified to think the boy might go into the cabin and destroy all the books and maps they'd brought with them than anything else that'd happened so far.

'Do you think you're able to travel, now?' Thordric asked him. He hadn't seen much of his friend over the past few days, partly because he'd been busy in the city, but mostly because he was ashamed of being the one who had caused his broken leg in the first place.

'I think so, the healer is quite impressed with how well I've done. He said that I should try to walk around using those sticks over there,' he replied, indicating two wooden canes with hand rests and a cuff that went around his upper arms for extra support. 'Apparently, I have to hop on one leg and use them to push me forwards as I do it.'

Thordric and Kal, knowing full well how clumsy Hamlet was, looked at each other. Having him try to do something like that wasn't a good idea; he would be in real danger of falling down and breaking his other leg.

'Maybe we'll support you between us,' Thordric said to

him, having a good mind to hide the sticks so that Hamlet wouldn't be able to try them.

'Well, if it won't be too inconvenient for you,' Hamlet said. 'When are we leaving, then?'

'At sunrise tomorrow,' Lyanis said, her voice wrought with the same determination to save the boy from the Shadow Seeker that Thordric felt.

2 0

KAL STEPS UP

The wagon thudded along the plains as the sun began to rise, sending clouds of birds up into the sky.

Thordric had found the gold tribe's stables filled with something close to the super oats, a special magic-enriched food mix for horses which aided their endurance, which were available in Dinia. They made sure their horses had eaten ample amounts before they'd left, but even so, Thordric was adamant that they stop for each night to give the horses some much needed rest. He didn't want to cause any more deaths by working them too hard.

He'd also asked both tribes if they could spare any food from their stores, seeing as the boy would have eaten a great deal of what was left on *Dinia's Jewel*, and the journey to get back to where it was anchored would take several days. Although some of the tribespeople objected due to what happened during the battle, most of them obliged because of how well the group had managed to fix everything afterwards.

The wagon, which Thordric was driving, was loaded with it all: different breads made from various grains, several large bunches of vegetables including carrots, potatoes and something that resembled turnips but wasn't. They also had a special fungus with them that was the same consistency as meat and contained the same nutrients, as all the real meat had spoilt because the gold tribe had forgotten to cure it during their battle preparations. Lyanis felt that eating the fungus was a good deal better and ate her meals without any suspicion that someone had accidentally put meat in them.

The last thing Thordric had made sure of before leaving was for the gold tribe and the black tribe to make a pact with each other so they would no longer fight, and perhaps even set up trade with each other. However, the black tribe decided to leave for their camp shortly afterwards to tell their children and mothers-to-be all that had happened.

On the third day, Thordric and the others finally reached *Dinia's Jewel*. Dismounting from the wagon, knowing full well that the black tribe would take care of the horses as soon as they passed through, they walked up to the ship. They spotted the boy as he peered at them over the side, crying silently. As he saw Lyanis, he said something to her in the guttural language of Wyotis and cried even more, but she simply laughed and replied back in Dinian.

'It's no good trying to make us feel sorry for you; we're the ones who trapped you like this in the first place. Besides, we know full well what you are,' she said.

The boy stopped crying and his face grew serious. They saw the tell-tale flicker of the Shadow Seeker in his eyes, fast and intense. 'I suppose you got hold of Sulvarda and made him talk, didn't you? He always was weak,' he said, all traces of his child-like innocence fleeing from his demeanour. 'What do you want with me?'

'I want you to leave that child's body so that he may live a normal life,' Lyanis said, her eyes steely.

The boy laughed. 'A normal life? No human ever wants just a normal life. They crave to be known, to do things that make others look up to them in awe. I have already done so for this boy; why would he possibly want to live a normal life after that?'

'You're wrong,' Kal said, stepping forwards to stand beside Lyanis, looking the boy defiantly in the eyes. 'I used to want to be known for my powers, to be known that I was my father's son, no matter how awful he was. I've tried many times to get people to notice my abilities, and I caused a lot of accidents without meaning to. Yet my friends at the Wizard Council, even though they tease me a lot, have always helped me make up for it afterwards. They've supported me every day since I've been there...though I've only realised that recently.'

He looked around at the others and bowed his head to them.

Seeing his student understand this brought a lump to Thordric's throat, and he knew that from now on, Kal would be able to control his hunger for magic and save himself from becoming like Kalljard.

Kal turned back to the boy. 'I've learnt that it's far better to have a normal life among friends than to be above them and have no one. This boy deserves the same chance to realise that, if he hasn't done so already,' he said.

'What nonsense,' the boy said in disgust. 'The whole reason you humans are so easy to manipulate is *because* of your hunger for more. The people who invaded our home were not content with simply settling down in one part; they wanted the whole country for themselves.'

'Greed is a human trait, indeed,' Lyanis said calmly to him. 'But in my own observations I have seen that they can rise above it if they truly wish. Had you have realised this instead of spurring them into battle and fuelling their need to be dominant over each other, then you may have been able to make them understand that they were causing your species to suffer. You could have had them help you and formed a relationship with them that would have benefited you both. But you did not, and now you alone remain of the Shadow Seekers.'

The boy said nothing and turned away from them. It was Thordric's turn to speak up.

'Leave the boy's body, and I will release the shield keeping you in. We will not harm you if you promise to stay away from humans for the rest of your life,' he said.

'There would be no point in that, for like my brother before me, I will also die soon. The true meaning of this battle was to decide which of us was superior before we left this world. Since I have survived much longer, I am the victor. I merely wished to escape so that I could live the rest of my days in peace, but I have used up too much of my energy now.'

The boy closed his eyes, and Thordric, realising that he was about to do the same as his brother, hurtled his magic into the boy's head and forced the Shadow Seeker out before he could kill the boy along with him. They saw a translucent blackness leave the boy's body, dispersing into the air moments after.

Thordric released the reverse shield over the ship and rushed up the ladder onto the deck, followed by the others. The boy had collapsed, but when they reached him, they found that he was still breathing. Thordric checked around his neck to see if his body was damaged like the little girl's had been, but it was fine. The boy was going to be alright.

They remained with him until the black tribe arrived to pick up their wagon. They found the boy had no memories at all, not even knowing of the magic inside his body. As he had no family that they knew of, they asked the black tribe if they could take him with them. The tribe agreed and went on their way, leaving Thordric, Ourellus, Hamlet, Kal and Lyanis to board *Dinia's Jewel* and set off, sailing back to Dinia.

It'd been a long journey travelling to all four countries surrounding Dinia, and now they were headed home, everyone realised how exhausted they were, and so took turns sleeping and steering the ship.

On the evening of the first day, however, as they passed the black pillars marking the border into Dinia, Thordric woke up. He could feel the intensity of the magic within it. It was very evident this time, now that the Ugamba's magic had fully settled with the other three, and he could feel the creature trapped within the pillar pulsing angrily. Though the spell on it felt strong, the creature was almost breaking through, and in a few months, it would be free again.

He knew that the first job he had to do once they'd restored Vey to his normal, unfrozen self was to strengthen all the pillars to make sure that the creatures remained sealed inside, at least until they could decide what to do about them.

As dawn broke a few days later, Thordric woke up again and saw Kal sitting next to him, reading. Kal glanced back and sniggered, noticing that Thordric's hair and beard were sticking up at odd angles.

'I think you need a haircut,' he said, still laughing as Thordric unravelled himself from his blankets.

'Speak for yourself,' Thordric replied, nodding to Kal's dreadlocks, which had grown considerably longer since they'd first set out. He stretched, yawning, and got up to rummage around in the food bags, looking for some nuts they'd been given in Wyotis. He found them and sat back down, eating silently.

'You know,' he said, after a while, 'that speech you gave was really something.'

Kal's brow creased, unsure if he was making fun of him, but Thordric's eyes were serious. 'Well, it was all true,' Kal replied as a pink tinge crept into his cheeks.

Thordric noticed. 'You shouldn't be embarrassed about it. It was something you needed to learn, and I'm very glad that you did.'

'I don't see how you can tell him not to be embarrassed by something like that when you can't even bring yourself to call Ourellus "father",' Lyanis smirked, leaning over Thordric's shoulder. She shot a look at Ourellus. 'You're as bad,' she said to him.

Both Thordric and Ourellus flushed pink themselves and looked away from each other at exactly the same time. Lyanis and Kal laughed, making Hamlet pop his head around the cabin door to see what was going on. But at that moment, Teroosa Forest came into sight.

Steering the ship to float just above the ground on the outskirts of the forest, Ourellus released the ladder and they all climbed down, taking in the smell of the trees – and of Dinia in general – that they realised they'd missed so much.

Hamlet had wanted to stay onboard so that he didn't slow them down with his broken leg, but Thordric told him it was nonsense to have travelled with them all the way and not be there when Vey woke up.

Thordric and Kal supported him between them while Lyanis and Ourellus led the way to the clearing where Vey was. They reached it after a little over two hours, though in their eagerness to get there, it'd felt more like four.

Vey was there, unharmed as Lyanis had promised them, with the same surprised expression still frozen on his face. Thordric took a deep breath. Now it was time to find out if their journey to gather the four magics had paid off.

He went up to Vey, feeling the frozen in time spell on him clearly. This was not a spell that he could undo by accident or without thinking, like when he'd mended the city walls in Wyotis. Breaking this one would require him to focus, because it wasn't purely Vey's life he was working with, it was Lyanis's magic too, along with the sealed powers of who knew how many women in the country.

Taking a deep breath, he poured his magic out towards Vey, using it to pick apart the spell bit by bit. It was easier to control now he was used to it, and he gradually felt it wearing away the first part of the spell – the trap that could bounce onto him if he did the wrong thing. Feeling the last few bits of it melt away, he exhaled, noting that he'd been holding his breath all along. Now he could get to the real work.

Making sure he was breathing properly, he turned his mind to the rest of the spell. As he reached into it, time seemed to slow down around him, until he got to the heart of the spell, where it stopped altogether. Thordric then understood that the only way to reverse the spell was to start time flowing again.

He pictured the clock above his desk back at the council. The pendulum was still, but then he made it swing, gently at first and then gaining momentum. He saw the hands on the clock face begin to move, the second hand ticking. Tick, tick, tick, tick.

Keeping that image firmly in his mind, he willed the time within the spell to follow it, ticking forwards along with the pendulum. It took a moment for it to take hold, but once it did, Thordric felt the spell disintegrating rapidly. Then it was gone.

Vey's body, now limp, fell forwards and Thordric caught him before he hit the ground. 'Bring me one of those light globes,' he said quietly to Kal, taking off his cloak and resting it under Vey's head.

Kal rushed over with one and held it up so they could all

see properly. Vey's eyes flickered under his eyelids, and he coughed. Thordric took out his water flask and unscrewed the cap, pouring a few drops onto Vey's lips. He managed to swallow and opened his eyes.

'Thordric?' he asked, his voice husky. Thordric gave him some more water, which he drank down greedily. 'What happened? I feel as though I've been asleep for days.'

'The spell you tried to undo had a trap on it. It transferred the spell to you, and you've been frozen in time for over a month,' Thordric explained, helping him sit up.

Vey looked at him, slightly dazed. 'Were you the one who broke it?' he asked, wonder in his expression.

'Yes, but I gathered the four magics from Wyotis, Numteqa, Fyoras and Uoo that Kalljard had within him when he first cast the spell,' Thordric said. 'It was the only way to do it.'

Vey's eyes widened, and he glanced around and saw everyone else there. He smiled at Hamlet and Kal, but as his gaze travelled to Ourellus and Lyanis, he looked puzzled. 'I know you,' he said to them. 'You were both frozen here origi-nally, weren't you?'

Before they could answer, however, Lyanis fell to the ground, gasping slightly. 'I'm alright,' she said, waving Thordric away as he made to dash over to her. 'It's my magic flowing back into my body now that the spell is broken.' Around her, the ground, which had been covered in dead leaves and twigs, was coming to life, sprouting flowers and delicate curled ferns.

'What a curious young woman,' Vey said, but then stopped. Behind her, walking out into the clearing, was another woman, similar to Lyanis but distinctly different.

Lyanis raised her head. 'I'm sorry,' she said to her. 'I didn't know you were trapped as well.'

21

MAGIC UNLEASHED!

Thordric examined the young woman curiously. She and Lyanis obviously knew each other, but he was sure she hadn't been in the forest earlier, at least not near the clearing where they were now.

'Who are you?' he asked her politely. She turned to him and smiled, making him blush like Lyanis had when he'd first met her. He wondered if that was a gift all female forest dwellers had.

Next to him, he noticed that Vey was entranced by her, and flushed so deep a crimson that he had to look away. Thordric suppressed a snigger.

'My name is Ilyu,' she said, her voice higher than Lyanis's. She gazed around at them all, her eyes bright and alert, as if she was etching every detail of them into her mind.

They waited for her to say more, but she looked to Lyanis to explain. 'Ilyu is the next protector of this forest. Before Kall-jard froze me in time, I poured some of my magic into the forest, with enough to start growing another forest dweller to take over, as I wanted to be prepared, in case he did try to get me out of the way. I knew he wasn't happy with me, so what he did wasn't unexpected. I thought that the amount of magic I used would be plenty to let Ilyu grow and keep the forest alive at the same time. Yet clearly, I was wrong,' Lyanis explained.

Ilyu softly inclined her head. 'I was formed slowly, my awareness only waking fully about forty years ago, but I was unable to emerge from my chrysalis. When Lyanis received her magic again, it poured more energy into the forest, and I was able to break free of it. It has been a long wait, and I have heard much that I could do nothing about,' she said.

'So, you've heard all the goings on in this forest for the past forty years?' Thordric asked her in surprise.

'Yes. I heard a man come here and release Ourellus some time ago. Patrick, I think his name was. He wanted to release Lyanis as well, but he could feel that the magic was too strong for him. He and Ourellus left and for over a year the forest was quiet, barely surviving, yet living peacefully otherwise. Then I heard the wizard, Kalljard, come to the forest with Ourellus. There was a struggle, and Ourellus was frozen again. More years passed after that, without anyone coming here, but then, nearly two months ago, a young man stumbled upon Ourellus and Lyanis. He was awfully excited if I recall,' she said, her eyes travelling over to Hamlet.

Hamlet grinned at her stupidly, not showing even the slightest trace of embarrassment. She smiled at him, too, and he blushed almost as deep a crimson as Vey had done.

'I suppose you heard Hamlet and Vey return and free Ourellus again, then?' Thordric asked.

'Yes, and the trap magic from Kalljard's spell on Lyanis take hold of Vey before Hamlet left the forest with Ourellus following him not long after. Then, of course, I heard you come here, Thordric, along with the others. You freed Lyanis, knowing that the spell on her had been weakened. I overheard everything said that day, so I knew you would soon return and free me from my chrysalis along with Vey and Lyanis's magic. I must thank you for that,' she said, dropping low to her knees and bowing her head.

'That's not, er, necessary,' Thordric said awkwardly, but Vey spoke up beside him.

'No, you and everyone else have journeyed and put yourselves in danger in order to do this, and we should both thank you all deeply for it,' he said, easing himself up onto both feet. He went over to Ilyu and took her hand to help her up. She looked at him quizzically but said nothing. Then he bowed low to everyone, his shoulder-length hair hanging down in front of his face.

'Now,' he said, standing up and flicking his hair back. A few strands stuck out, and Ilyu started to brush them back into place with her hand. She stopped quickly as she noticed Lyanis looking at her with an amused expression.

'I don't mean to break up the moment,' said Kal, rubbing his hands together and breathing on them, the chill morning air making them cold and stiff. 'But could we continue this back at the council? It's nice and warm there, and I'm sure Lizzie and the others would want to know that we've succeeded.'

'What's this?' Vey asked, his eyebrow shooting up at the mention of Lizzie's name. 'What's my mother doing at the Wizard Council?'

'I put her in charge while we were away.' Thordric shrugged like it was obvious.

Vey simply stared at him.

When they arrived back at the council, with Lyanis, Ilyu and Ourellus coming with them at Vey's insistence, they found it in an uproar.

Thordric and Vey rushed in to see what the matter was, and found Lizzie trying to calm down Thordric's mother, Maggie, who was holding her two young daughters at arm's length due to the flames sprouting out of their hands. The inspector was with her, trying not to get too close to their flames despite how hard they were trying to grab him.

'Thordric!' his mother cried, seeing him. 'I'm so glad you're back – the twins, I didn't know what to do, they just started...' She made a wild gesture that he guessed was meant to represent their fire covered hands.

'It's alright, mother,' Thordric said, rushing over to them, with Vey sprinting along behind. The High Wizard was looking at the twins in utter confusion.

'I don't understand,' he said, not hearing the cries of joy coming from Lizzie and the other Council wizards at his safe return. 'They're girls...but unless my eyes are deceiving me, those are magical flames.'

Thordric couldn't help but grin. 'They are. I had a feeling something like this would happen, though not with my own sisters.'

Lizzie, after embracing Vey tightly, turned to Thordric. 'You have an explanation for all of this, then?' she asked.

'It's merely their magic coming out, like how it does with every other wizard—'

'But Thordric, they're *girls*. They can't have magic!' the inspector said, still dodging their flaming hands.

'Actually, I think you'll find a lot of girls and women will be coming in like this after today. It's not that women have never had magic. According to what Lyanis says, they always used to, but it was sealed away along with hers when Kalljard froze her in time a thousand years ago and—'

He was cut off suddenly as his mother broke in.

'Who's this Lyanis?' she asked suspiciously. 'And why have you never mentioned her before?'

'She's a forest dweller, and also my grandmother,' he said without thinking.

'Grandmother?' she said, disbelievingly. 'But she's been dead for nearly sixteen years, and her name was Winona, not Lyanis.'

'No, mother,' he said, realising his mistake and deciding to tell her the truth anyway. 'Not your mother, but...father's mother.'

Her eyes grew wide, and at that moment the others came into the hall. She took one look at Ourellus and shrieked, letting go of the twins in shock. They immediately ran after the inspector, accidentally setting fire to the drapes as they went.

Vey acted quickly and put the flames out with his magic, levitating the twins up high so that they couldn't cause anymore havoc.

'Mummy, mummy, High Wizard Vey's being mean to us!' Elle cried, as both the flames on her hands and her sister, Mae's, sputtered and went out.

Vey looked at Thordric. 'Did you extinguish them?' he asked, knowing that subduing freshly awakened magic was extremely difficult.

Thordric tried not to look smug. 'Handy, this new magic of mine,' he said.

'What's the problem now?' the inspector asked, catching his breath, and looking over at Thordric's mother, who was still gazing at Ourellus in horror. He was staring back at her, unsure what to say.

'He's...he's...'

'He's my father,' Thordric said for her.

'Don't be silly, boy, he can only be a few years older than

yourself,' the inspector said, uncertain of whether Thordric was joking or not.

'You must be Maggie's new husband,' Ourellus managed at last, guessing who the inspector was. 'I know these are incredibly peculiar circumstances, but Thordric is telling the truth. I am his father.'

The inspector turned slowly from him to Thordric's mother. Her expression confirmed what Ourellus had said.

'I think I need a large cup of tea and some Jaffa cakes,' the inspector breathed, dumbstruck.

'Perhaps it would be best if we continued this up in my chambers,' Vey suggested, as he noticed every ear in the room tuned in to their conversation. 'Thordric, would you take everyone up? I'll join you shortly.'

Thordric did so, hearing Vey address the rest of the council as they left, beginning to explain what had happened. Once everyone was inside Vey's room, Thordric's mother cried out at Ourellus.

'How could you do this to me? I thought that you'd abandoned me. Or worse,' she said, unable to bear looking at him.

'It's not his fault, Maggie,' Lizzie said calmly.

Maggie turned on her. 'You knew who he was?' she said, her eyes hard.

'I didn't know his relationship to you, nor, until these past two months, did I know *exactly* who he was. However, we had met before,' Lizzie replied, taking a deep breath. 'Maggie, Ourellus is Kalljard's older brother. He and his mother, Lyanis the forest dweller, were frozen in time by Kalljard a thousand years ago. Then, just over twenty years ago, my husband, Patrick, managed to free him. I presume it was at that time he met you.'

'Yes, it was,' Ourellus said quietly. 'After I met you, Maggie, I had every intention of staying with you, but my brother found out that I'd been freed and came after me again. He took me back to the forest and froze me in time, as he'd done before. That is why I never returned to you.'

Maggie gazed at him, tears rolling down her face as her memories of that time shone in her eyes, but the inspector was concerned with other matters.

'Now, look here, boy,' he said to Ourellus, his overly active moustache curling up to his nostrils. 'I hope you haven't come back thinking that you can get involved in my wife's life again.'

Ourellus stepped back, holding his arms up and shaking his head, alarmed by the inspector's sudden reaction. 'No, no. I never had any such thoughts. I know it's been too long for that.'

'Good,' the inspector replied, calming down. 'I hope you remember that.'

The door opened and Vey came in, looking harassed. 'I thought I'd never shake them off,' he said, pulling up a chair for himself.

'They were terribly concerned about you. You *are* High Wizard, after all,' Lizzie reprimanded him.

Vey was about to say something back, but then saw Ilyu watching him and shut his mouth abruptly, going crimson again. Lizzie eyed him suspiciously.

'Now we've got the matter of Ourellus cleared up; though I'm sure you still all have much to talk about; can I ask who this young lady standing next to Lyanis is and why we have two young girls able to use magic?' Lizzie said, still glancing at Vey as he looked at Ilyu. There was a smile playing about her lips as she spoke, though Thordric was sure he was the only one who'd noticed it.

'One of those women is this Lyanis?' Thordric's mother asked, snapping out of her shock, and scrutinizing them both, trying to work out which one she was.

Lyanis stepped forwards. 'I am Lyanis,' she said. 'It is true that I am Thordric's grandmother, and also Kal's, and so the mother of Ourellus and Kalljard too.'

Thordric's mother blinked at her. 'But you're so young!' she exclaimed.

'Forest dwellers don't age the same as humans,' she said with a shrug. 'That, and I've been frozen in time longer than Ourellus. Now, in answer to your questions, Lizzie, the young forest dweller beside me is Ilyu, and will be the next protector of Teroosa Forest. She was trapped in her chrysalis until Thordric broke the spell on Vey and my magic was released along with it. That is the reason why these two girls are now showing signs of magic. When Kalljard froze me, he also put a powerful seal on my magic, which was then transferred to Vey with the trapping spell after he tried to free me. However, Kalljard cast the spell so strongly that he unknowingly sealed away the magic of all women. As Thordric explained earlier, there are just as many women born with magic as men are, but because of Kalljard's spell, no one realised it because their magic was sealed for all these years.'

Lizzie had been listening to her quietly, but then spoke up. 'Strange as it is for me to think it, that makes a surprising amount of sense. I've always wondered why it was that only men were sometimes born with magic.'

Thordric noticed there was sadness in her eyes. Without knowing it, he'd expected to find that she was able to use magic too, as she knew so much about it.

Lyanis also seemed to pick up on her sorrow, for she said gently, 'You may still show signs of it yet. The spell has only been broken a few hours. Give it time.'

'You've wanted to use magic, mother?' Vey said, surprised.

'Only because I know it would have pleased your father,' she said, smiling again. 'And it would probably be useful to have, every now and then.'

'You know,' Hamlet said to Kal, both of them standing quietly in the corner, 'with all these family reunions going on, I almost feel left out.'

'Nonsense,' Lizzie and Lyanis snapped at him together.

'You're as much a part of this, er, ever growing family as the rest of us,' Vey added, clapping him on the shoulder.

The twins also thought the same, for they ran up to him and promptly set the cast on his leg on fire, giggling happily. Thordric quickly put it out, and everyone laughed. It was good to be home.

2 2

ILYU'S CHOICE

Thordric stood facing the last onyx pillar along Dinia's east boundary, finally having strengthened the spells on all of them to keep the creatures inside from escaping.

It'd been six months since the day they'd all returned to the Wizard Council, and so much had happened since then that he was absolutely exhausted.

True to his prediction, the council had been swamped with women of all ages coming to them in a panic, saying that they'd suddenly developed magical powers. Vey had been busy explaining to them all why it was happening, as well as extending the Wizard Council Training Facility to accommodate as many of them as he could, telling the other wizards to clean up their rooms now that there were ladies present.

Lizzie, Thordric had been pleased to hear, had eventually shown signs of magic, and trained herself so quickly that she was now a match for any of the wizards who had been part of the council for years. She also promised to train Thordric's little sisters, as neither Thordric's mother nor the inspector could bring themselves to let them live at the Training Facility.

Ourellus had also been made part of the council by Vey, and had been spending most of his time in the library, trying to catch up on everything he'd missed while he'd been frozen. Hamlet, now fully recovered, had been helping him, as well as giving lengthy lectures on all the archaeological discoveries he'd made so far.

Among all of this, Vey, to no one's real surprise, proposed to Ilyu and planned to marry her a week after Thordric was due to return. Lyanis announced she was content to look after Teroosa Forest jointly with Ilyu if the younger forest dweller was truly set on marriage. However, she explained to both of them that it would not be easy to spend their lives together, what with Ilyu remaining ageless while Vey grew older.

However, after finding out about Thordric's new powers, Ilyu had approached him about the prospect of turning her human.

Thordric thought it doubtful, but Ilyu had urged him to try. So, he'd passed most of the time travelling from one pillar to the next by studying human anatomy. There was a lot to learn, but it finally felt as though he knew enough to give it a shot.

He sighed and boarded *Dinia's Jewel*, making his way back to Teroosa Forest, where he knew Ilyu was waiting.

Making good time and landing on the outskirts of the forest just after sunrise the next morning, he climbed down the ladder onto the ground, seeing her and Lyanis standing there together.

'I'll warn you, I have no idea if this will work or not,' he said to Ilyu uncertainly.

'I believe you can do it, and so does Vey,' she replied, looking straight into his eyes.

'And you're absolutely sure about this? Once this is done, there's no going back, because I simply don't know enough about forest dwellers to do it,' he said.

'I know. I've made my choice. I want to live with Vey as a human so that we may age together,' she said decisively.

'Alright, then,' Thordric breathed. 'Here it goes.'

He summoned his magic within him, drawing on every inch of it, and sent it pouring into Ilyu's body. Drawing on all the knowledge of human anatomy he'd learnt, he kept a firm picture of her being human in his mind. It took so much effort that he closed his eyes, but after minutes of struggling, it was done. He opened them again and studied her. Where her skin had been silvery grey like Lyanis's, it was now a soft coffee colour, and her hair, which had been the shade of moss, was a deep, rich auburn.

His magic had worked. She was human.

With delight, she span around on the spot and looking at her hands and legs. He pulled a mirror out of his pocket and gave it to her. She squealed with happiness when she saw her reflection and hugged him tightly.

'Thank you, thank you,' she said breathlessly, unable to think of anything else to say to him, for nothing quite expressed how she felt. 'Will you take me back to the council with you?' she asked once she'd calmed down a bit more. He nodded, feeling utterly drained. 'I'll meet you onboard the ship, then,' she said, speeding off and leaving him to sit on the forest floor next to Lyanis.

'What will you do now she's human?' Thordric asked her, knowing that the forest dweller now had no replacement.

'I will remain looking after this forest for a time, long enough to grow another forest dweller who wants to take over from me. After that, I imagine I shall linger in town for a while, before leaving this world.'

He sat up, gawping at her. 'You mean you'll die?'

She cocked her head to the side. 'Perhaps, but I am not yet certain. In truth, I do not know what happens to forest dwellers who choose to permanently leave their forests. I was always told that death was the fate of those who did, but whether there is any accuracy in that, I am unsure. After all, we are bonded to the forest, and as long as the forest lives on, so should we.'

She watched him relax after hearing her explanation. 'What is it you plan to do with *your* time now?' she asked, intrigued.

'Well, after I attend Vey and Ilyu's wedding, I suppose I'd better get back to training Kal and working on the dishwashing spell I started before all this happened.'

She laughed at him, and after a few seconds, he understood why. After everything he'd done recently, making his dishwashing spell work would be easy.

Dear reader,

We hope you enjoyed reading *Unseasoned Adventurer*. Please take a moment to leave a review, even if it's a short one. Your opinion is important to us.

Discover more books by Kathryn Wells at https://www. nextchapter.pub/authors/kathryn-wells-fantasy-author

Want to know when one of our books is free or discounted? Join the newsletter at http://eepurl.com/bqqB3H

Best regards,
Kathryn Wells and the Next Chapter Team

ABOUT THE AUTHOR

Kathryn Wells is the pen name of author Kathryn Rossati, a writer of fantasy, children's fiction, short stories, and poetry.

As a child, she found her passion for the written word, and even though she had many other interests growing up, writing was always the one she would return to.

Her favourite authors are Diana Wynne Jones, Geanna Culbertson, Suzanne Collins, Jonathan Stroud, Neil Gaiman, Garth Nix, and David Eddings, to name but a few.

You can find more information about Kathryn on her website:

http://www.kathrynrossati.co.uk

BOOKS BY THE AUTHOR

Printed in Great Britain
by Amazon